SHOWDOWN TRAIL

Center Point
Large Print

Also by Louis L'Amour and available from Center Point Large Print:

The Trail to Crazy Man
Riders of the Dawn

This Large Print Book carries the Seal of Approval of N.A.V.H.

SHOWDOWN TRAIL

A WESTERN TRIO

LOUIS L'AMOUR

CENTER POINT LARGE PRINT
THORNDIKE, MAINE

This Circle Ⓥ Western is published by
Center Point Large Print in the year 2019 in
co-operation with Golden West Literary Agency.

Copyright © 2019 by Golden West Literary Agency.

March 2019
First Edition

Printed in the United States of America
on permanent paper.
Set in 16-point Times New Roman type.

ISBN: 978-1-64358-133-0

Library of Congress Cataloging-in-Publication Data

Names: L'Amour, Louis, 1908-1988, author. | L'Amour, Louis,
    1908-1988. Black Rock. | L'Amour, Louis, 1908-1988.
    Gamble of the KT. | L'Amour, Louis, 1908-1988. Showdown Trail.
Title: Showdown trail : a western trio / Louis L'Amour.
Other titles: Black Rock. | Gamble of the KT. | Showdown Trail.
Description: First edition. | Thorndike, Maine : Center Point Large Print,
    2019. | Series: A Circle V western | Black Rock originally
    published as The Black Rock coffin makers.
Identifiers: LCCN 2018056898 | ISBN 9781643581330
    (hardcover : large print : alk. paper)
Subjects: LCSH: Large type books.
Classification: LCC PS3523.A446 A6 2019 | DDC 813/.52—dc23
LC record available at https://lccn.loc.gov/2018056898

19\03

ACKNOWLEDGMENTS

"Black Rock" first appeared under the title "The Black Rock Coffin Makers" in *.44 Western* (2/50). Copyright © 1950 by Popular Publications, Inc. Copyright not renewed.

"Gamble of the KT" first appeared under the title "Shandy Takes a Hook" in *Texas Rangers* (10/51). Copyright © 1951 by Better Publications Inc. Copyright not renewed.

"Showdown Trail" first appeared under the title "Showdown on the Hogback" in *Giant Western* (8/50). Copyright © 1950 by Best Publications, Inc. Copyright not renewed.

TABLE OF CONTENTS

SHOWDOWN TRAIL

BLACK ROCK

I

Jim Gatlin had been up the creek and over the mountains, and more than once had been on both ends of a six-shooter. Lean and tall, with shoulders wide for his height and a face like saddle leather, he was, at the moment, doing a workman-like job of demolishing the last of a thick steak and picking off isolated beans that had escaped his initial attack. He was a thousand miles from home and knew nobody in the town of Tucker.

He glanced up as the door opened and saw a short, thick-bodied man. The man gave one startled look at Jim and ducked back out of sight. Gatlin blinked in surprise, then shrugged and filled his coffee cup from the pot standing on the restaurant table.

Puzzled, he listened to the rapidly receding pound of a horse's hoofs, then rolled a smoke, sitting back with a contented sigh. Some two-hundred and fifty odd miles to the north was the herd he had drifted northwest from Texas. The money the cattle had brought was in the belt

11

around his waist and his pants pockets. Nothing remained now but to return to Texas, bank the profit, and pick up a new herd.

The outer door opened again, and a tall girl entered the restaurant. Turning right, she started for the door leading to the hotel. She stopped abruptly as though his presence had only then registered. She turned, and her eyes widened in alarm. Swiftly, she crossed the room to him.

"Are you insane?" she whispered. "Sitting here like that when the town is full of Wing Cary's hands? They know you're coming and have been watching for you for days."

Gatlin looked up, smiling. "Ma'am, you've sure got the wrong man, although if a girl as pretty as you is worried about him, he sure is a lucky fellow. I'm a stranger here. I never saw the place until an hour ago."

She stepped back, puzzled, and then the door slammed open once more, and a man stepped into the room. He was as tall as Jim, but thinner, and his dark eyes were angry. "Get away from him, Lisa! I'm killin' him . . . right now!"

The man's hand flashed for a gun, and Gatlin dived sidewise to the floor, drawing as he fell. A gun roared in the room, then Gatlin fired twice.

The tall man caught himself, jerking his left arm against his ribs, his face twisted as he gasped for breath. Then he wilted slowly to the floor, his gun sliding from his fingers.

Gatlin got to his feet, staring at the stranger. He swung his eyes to the girl staring at him. "Who is that *hombre*?" he snapped. "What's this all about? Who did he think I was?"

"You . . . you're not . . . you aren't Jim Walker?" Her voice was high, amazed.

"Walker?" He shook his head. "I'm sure as hell not. The name is Gatlin. I'm just driftin' through."

There was a rush of feet in the street outside. She caught his hand. "Come. Come quickly. They won't listen to you. They'll kill you. All the Cary outfit are in town."

She ran beside him, dodging into the hotel, and then swiftly down a hall. As the front door burst open, they plunged out the back and into the alley behind the building. Unerringly she led him to the left, and then opened the back door of another building and drew him inside. Silently she closed the door and stood closely beside him, panting in the darkness.

Shouts and curses rang from the building next door. A door banged, and men charged up and down outside. Jim was still holding his gun, but now he withdrew the empty shells and fed two into the cylinder to replace those fired. He slipped a sixth into the usually empty chamber. "What is this place?" he whispered. "Will they come here?"

"It's a law office," she whispered. "I work here

part time, and I left the door open myself. They'll not think of this place." Stealthily she lifted the bar and dropped it into place. "Better sit down. They'll be searching the streets for some time."

He found the desk and seated himself on the corner, well out of line with the windows. He could see only the vaguest outline of her face. His first impression of moments before was strong enough for him to remember she was pretty. The gray eyes were wide and clear, her figure rounded yet slim. "What is this?" he repeated. "What was he gunnin' for me for?"

"It wasn't you. He thought you were Jim Walker of the XY. If you aren't actually him, you look enough like him to be a brother, a twin brother."

"Where is he? What goes on here? Who was that *hombre* who tried to gun me down?"

She paused, and seemed to be thinking, and he had the idea she was still uncertain whether to believe him or not. "The man you killed was Bill Trout. He was the badman of Paradise country and *segundo* on Wing Cary's Flying C spread. Jim Walker called him a thief and a murderer in talking to Cary, and Trout threatened to shoot him on sight. Walker hasn't been seen since, and that was four days ago, so everybody believed Walker had skipped the country. Nobody blamed him much."

"What's it all about?" Gatlin inquired.

14

"North of here, up beyond Black Rock, is Alder Creek country, with some rich bottom hay land lying in several corners of the mountains. This is dry country, but that Alder Creek area has springs and some small streams flowing down out of the hills. The streams flow into the desert and die there, so the water is good only for the man who controls the range."

"And that was Walker?"

"No, up until three weeks ago, it was old Dave Butler. Then Dave was thrown from his horse and killed, and, when they read his will, he had left the property to be sold at auction and the money to be paid to his nephew and niece back in New York. However, the joke was, he stipulated that Jim Walker was to get the ranch if he would bid ten thousand cash and forty thousand on his note, payable in six years."

"In other words, he wanted Walker to have the property?" Jim asked. "He got first chance at it?"

"That's right. And I was to get second chance. If Jim didn't want to make the bid, I could have it for the same price. If neither of us wanted it, the ranch was to go on public auction, and that means that Cary and Horwick would get it. They have the money, and nobody around here could outbid them."

The street outside was growing quieter as the excitement of the chase died down. "I think," Lisa continued, "that Uncle Dave wanted Jim to have the property because Jim did so much to develop it. Jim was foreman of the XY acting for Dave. Then, Uncle Dave knew my father and liked me, and he knew I loved the ranch, so he wanted me to have second chance, but I don't have the money, and they all know it. Jim had some of it, and he could get the rest. I think that was the real issue behind his trouble with Trout. I believe Wing deliberately set Trout to kill him, and Jim's statements about Bill were a result of the pushing around Bill Trout had given him."

The pattern was not unfamiliar, and Gatlin could easily appreciate the situation. Water was gold in this country of sparse grass. To a cattleman, such a ranch as Lisa described could be second to none, with plenty of water and grass and good hay meadows. Suddenly she caught his arm. Men were talking outside the door.

"Looks like he got plumb away, Wing. Old Ben swears there was nobody in the room with him but that Lisa Cochrane, an' she never threw that gun, but how Jim Walker ever beat Trout is more'n I can see. Why, Bill was the fastest man around here unless it's you or me."

"That wasn't Walker, Pete. It couldn't have been."

"Ben swears it was, an' Woody Hammer busted right through the door in front of him. Said it was Jim, all right."

Wing Cary's voice was irritable. "I tell you,

it couldn't have been!" he flared. "Jim Walker never saw the day he dared face Trout with a gun. I've seen Walker draw an' he never was fast."

"Maybe he wasn't," Pete Chasin agreed dryly, "but Trout's dead, ain't he?"

"Three days left," Cary said. "Lisa Cochrane hasn't the money, and it doesn't look like Walker will even be bidding. Let it ride, Pete. I don't think we need to worry about anything. Even if that was Walker . . . an' I'd take an oath it wasn't . . . he's gone for good now. All we have to do is sit tight."

The two moved off, and Jim Gatlin, staring at the girl in the semidarkness, saw her lips were tightly pressed. His eyes had grown accustomed to the dim light, and he could see around the small office. It was a simple room with a desk, chair, and filing cabinets. Well-filled bookcases lined the walls.

He got to his feet. "I've got to get my gear out of that hotel," he said, "and my horse."

"You're leaving?" she asked.

Jim glanced at her in surprise. "Why, sure. Why stay here in a fight that's not my own? I've already killed one man, and, if I stay, I'll have to kill more or be killed myself. There's nothing here for me."

"Did you notice something?" she asked suddenly. "Wing Cary seemed very sure that Jim Walker wasn't coming back, that you weren't he."

Gatlin frowned. He had noticed it, and it had him wondering. "He did sound mighty sure. Like he might know Walker wasn't coming back."

They were silent in the dark office, yet each knew what the other was thinking. Jim Walker was dead. Pete Chasin had not known it. Neither, obviously, had Bill Trout.

"What happens to you then?" Gatlin asked suddenly. "You lose the ranch?"

She shrugged. "I never had it, and never really thought I would have it, only . . . well, if Jim had lived . . . I mean, if Jim got the ranch, we'd have made out. We were very close, like brother and sister. Now I don't know what I can do."

"You haven't any people?"

"None that I know of." Her head came up suddenly. "Oh, it isn't myself I'm thinking of, it's all the old hands, the ranch itself. Uncle Dave hated Cary, and so do his men. Now he'll get the ranch, and they'll all be fired, and he'll ruin the place. That's what he's wanted all along."

Gatlin shifted his feet. "Tough," he said, "mighty tough." He opened the door slightly. "Thanks," he said, "for getting me out of there."

She didn't reply, so after a moment he stepped out of the door and drew it gently to behind him.

There was no time to lose. He must be out of town by daylight and with miles behind him. There was no sense getting mixed up in somebody else's fight, for all he'd get out of it

18

would be a bellyful of lead. There was nothing he could do to help. He moved swiftly, and within a matter of minutes was in his hotel room. Apparently searching for Jim Walker, they hadn't considered his room in the hotel, so Gatlin got his duffel together, stuffed it into his saddlebags, and picked up his rifle. With utmost care, he eased down the back stairs and into the alley.

The streets were once more dark and still. What had become of the Flying C hands he didn't know, but none was visible. Staying on back streets, he made his way carefully to the livery barn, but there his chance of cover grew less, for he must enter the wide door with a light glowing over it.

After listening, he stepped out and, head down, walked through the door. Turning, he hurried to the stall where his powerful black waited. It was the work of only a few minutes to saddle up. He led the horse out of the stall and caught up the bridle. As his hand grasped the pommel, a voice stopped him.

"Lightin' out?"

It was Pete Chasin's voice. Slowly he released his grip on the pommel and turned slightly. The man was hidden in a stall.

"Why not?" Gatlin asked. "I'm not goin' to be a shootin' gallery for nobody. This ain't my range, an' I'm slopin' out of here for Texas. I'm no trouble hunter."

He heard Chasin's chuckle. "Don't reckon you are. But it seems a shame not to make the most of your chance. What if I offered you five thousand to stay? Five thousand, in cash?"

"Five thousand?" Gatlin blinked. That was half as much as he had in his belt, and the ten thousand he carried had taken much hard work and bargaining to get. Buying a herd, chancing the long drive.

"What would I have to do?" he demanded.

Chasin came out of the stall. "Be yourself," he said, "just be yourself . . . but let folks think you're Jim Walker. Then you buy a ranch here . . . I'll give you the money, an' then you hit the trail."

Chasin was trying to double-cross Cary? To get the ranch for himself?

Gatlin hesitated. "That's a lot of money, but these boys toss a lot of lead. I might not live to spend the dough."

"I'll hide you out," Chasin argued. "I've got a cabin in the hills. I'd hide you out with four or five of my boys to stand guard. You'd be safe enough. Then you could come down, put your money on the line, an' sign the papers."

"Suppose they want Walker's signature checked?"

"Jim Walker never signed more'n three, four papers in his life. He left no signatures hereabouts. I've took pains to be sure."

Five thousand dollars because he looked like a man. It was easy money, and he'd be throwing a monkey wrench into Wing Cary's plans. Cary, a man he'd decided he disliked. "Sounds like a deal," he said. "Let's go!"

The cabin on the north slope of Bartlett Peak was well hidden, and there was plenty of grub. Pete Chasin left him there with two men to guard him and two more standing by on the trail toward town. All through the following day, Jim Gatlin loafed, smoking cigarettes and talking idly with the two men. Hab Johnson was a big, unshaven *hombre* with a sullen face and a surly manner. He talked little, and then only to growl. Pink Stabineau was a wide-chested, flat-faced jasper with an agreeable grin.

Gatlin had a clear idea of his own situation. He could use the five thousand, but he knew Chasin never intended him to leave the country with it and doubted if he would last an hour after the ranch was transferred to Chasin himself. Yet Gatlin had been around the rough country, and he knew a trick or two of his own. Several times he thought of Lisa Cochrane, but avoided that angle as much as he could.

After all, she had no chance to get the ranch, and Walker was probably dead. That left it between Cary and Chasin. The unknown Horwick, of whom he had heard mention, was

21

around, too, but he seemed to stand with Cary in everything.

Yet Gatlin was restless and irritable, and he kept remembering the girl beside him in the darkness and her regrets at breaking up the old outfit. Jim Gatlin had been a hand who rode for the brand; he knew what it meant to have a ranch sold out from under a bunch of old hands. The home that had been theirs gone, the friends drifting apart never to meet again, everything changed.

He finished breakfast on the morning of the second day, then walked out of the cabin with his saddle. Hab Johnson looked up sharply. "Where you goin'?" he demanded.

"Ridin'," Gatlin said briefly, "an' don't worry. I'll be back."

Johnson chewed a stem of grass, his hard eyes on Jim's. "You ain't goin' nowheres. The boss said to watch you an' keep you here. Here you stay."

Gatlin dropped his saddle. "You aren't keepin' me nowhere, Hab," he said flatly. "I've had enough sittin' around. I aim to see a little of this country."

"I reckon not." Hab got to his feet. "You may be a fast hand with a gun, but you ain't gittin' both of us, and you ain't so foolish as to try." He waved a big hand. "Now you go back an' set down."

"I started for a ride," Jim said quietly, "and a

ride I'm takin'." He stooped to pick up the saddle and saw Hab's boots as the big man started for him. Jim had lifted the saddle clear of the ground, and now he hurled it, suddenly, in Hab's path. The big man stumbled and hit the ground on his hands and knees, then started up.

As he came up halfway, Jim slugged him. Hab tottered, fighting for balance, and Gatlin moved in, striking swiftly with a volley of lefts and rights to the head. Hab went down and hit hard, then came up with a lunge, but Gatlin dropped him again. Blood dripped from smashed lips and a cut on his cheek bone.

Gatlin stepped back, working his fingers. His hard eyes flicked to Pink Stabineau, who was smoking quietly, resting on one elbow, looking faintly amused. "You stoppin' me?" Gatlin demanded.

Pink grinned. "Me? Now where did you get an idea like that? Take your ride. Hab's just too persnickety about things. Anyway, he's always wantin' to slug somebody. Now maybe he'll be quiet for a spell."

There was a dim trail running northwest from the cabin and Gatlin took it, letting his horse choose his own gait. The black was a powerful animal, not only good on a trail but an excellent roping horse, and he moved out eagerly, liking the new country. When Gatlin had gone scarcely more than two miles, he skirted the edge of a high meadow with plenty of grass, then left the trail and turned off along a bench of the mountain, riding due north.

Suddenly the mountain fell away before him, and below, in a long finger of grass, he saw the silver line of a creek, and nestled against a shoulder of the mountain he discerned roofs among the trees. Pausing, Jim rolled a smoke and studied the lay of the land. Northward, for all of ten miles, there was good range. Dry, but not so bad as over the mountain, and in the spring and early summer it would be good grazing land. He had looked at too much range not to detect from the colors of the valley before him some of the varieties of grass and brush. Northwest, the range stretched away through a wide gap in the mountains, and he seemed to distinguish a deeper green in the distance.

Old Dave Butler had chosen well, and his XY had been well handled, Gatlin could see as he rode nearer. Tanks had been built to catch some of the overflow from the mountains and to prevent the washing away of valuable range. The old man, and evidently Jim Walker, had worked hard to build this ranch into something. Even while wanting money for his relatives in the East, Butler had tried to ensure that the work would be continued after his death. Walker would continue it, and so would Lisa Cochrane.

II

All morning he rode, and well into the afternoon, studying the range but avoiding the buildings. Once, glancing back, he saw a group of horsemen riding swiftly out of the mountains from which he had come and heading for the XY. Reining in, he watched from a vantage point among some huge boulders. Men wouldn't ride that fast without adequate reason.

Morosely, he turned and started back along the way he had come, thinking more and more of Lisa. Five thousand was a lot of money, but what he was doing was not dishonest, and so far he had played the game straight. Still, why think of that? In a few days, he'd have the money in his pocket and be headed for Texas. He turned on the brow of the hill and glanced back, carried away despite himself by the beauty of the wide sweep of range.

Pushing on, he skirted around and came toward the cabin where he had been staying, off from the town trail. He was riding with his mind far away when the black snorted violently and shied. Jim drew up, staring at the man who lay sprawled in the trail. It was the cowhand Pete Chasin had left on guard there. He'd been shot through the stomach, and a horse had been ridden over him.

Swinging down, a quick check showed that the man was dead. Jim grabbed up the reins and sprang into the saddle. Sliding a six-gun from its holster, he pushed forward, riding cautiously. The tracks told him that a party of twelve horsemen had come this way.

He heard the wind in the trees, the distant cry of an eagle, but nothing more. He rode out into the clearing before the cabin, and drew up. Another man had died here. It wasn't Stabineau or Hab Johnson, but the other guard, who must have retreated to this point for aid.

Gun in hand, Gatlin pushed the door open and looked into the cabin. Everything was smashed, yet when he swung down and went in, he found his own gear intact, under the overturned bed. He threw his bedroll on his horse and loaded up his saddlebags. He jacked a shell into the chamber of the Winchester and was about to mount up when he heard a muffled cry.

Turning, he stared around, then detected a faint stir among the leaves of a mountain mahogany. Warily, he walked over and stepped around the bush.

Pink Stabineau, his face pale and his shirt dark with blood, lay sprawled on the ground. Curiously there was still a faint touch of humor in his eyes when he looked up at Gatlin. "Got me," he said finally. "It was that damned Hab. He sold us out . . . to Wing Cary. The damn' dirty . . . !"

Jim dropped to his knees and gently unbuttoned the man's shirt. The wound was low down on the left side, and, although he seemed to have lost much blood, there was a chance. Working swiftly, he built a fire, heated water, and bathed, and then dressed the wound. From time to time, Pink talked, telling him much of what he suspected, that Cary would hunt Chasin down now and kill him.

"If they fight," Jim asked, "who'll win?"

Stabineau grinned wryly. "Cary . . . he's tough, an' cold as ice. Pete's too jumpy. He's fast, but, mark my words, if they face each other, he'll shoot too fast and miss his first shot. Wing won't miss. But it won't come to that. Wing's a cinch player. He'll chase him down an' the bunch will gun him to death. Wing's bloodthirsty."

Leaving food and a canteen of water beside the wounded man and giving him two blankets, Jim Gatlin mounted. His deal was off then. The thought left him with a distinct feeling of relief. He had never liked any part of it, and he found himself without sympathy for Pete Chasin. The man had attempted a double-cross and failed.

Well, the road was open again now, and there was nothing between him and Texas but the miles. Yet he hesitated, and then turned his horse toward the XY. He rode swiftly, and at sundown was at the ranch. He watched it for a time, and saw several hands working around, yet there seemed little activity. No doubt they were waiting to see what was to happen.

Suddenly a sorrel horse started out from the ranch and swung into the trail toward town. Jim Gatlin squinted his eyes against the fading glare of the sun and saw the rider was a woman. That would be Lisa Cochrane.

Suddenly he swung the black and, touching spurs to the horse, raced down the mountain to intercept her.

Until that moment, he had been uncertain as to the proper course, but now he knew. Yet for all his speed, his eyes were alert and watchful, for he realized the risk he ran. Wing Cary would be quick to discover that as long as he was around and alive, there was danger, and even now the rancher might have his men out, scouring the country for him. Certainly there were plausible reasons enough, for it could be claimed that he had joined with Chasin in a plot to get the ranch by pretending to be Jim Walker.

Lisa's eyes widened when she saw him. "I thought you'd be gone by now. There's a posse after you."

"You mean some of Cary's men?" he corrected.

"I mean a posse. Wing has men on your trail, too, but they lost you somehow. He claims that you were tied up in a plan with Pete Chasin to get the ranch, and that you killed Jim Walker."

His eyes searched her face. "You mean he actually claims that?"

She nodded, watching him. "He says that story about your being here was all nonsense, that you actually came on purpose, that you and Chasin rigged it that way. You'll have to admit it looks funny, you arriving right at this time and looking just like Jim."

"What if it does?" he demanded impatiently. "I never heard of Jim Walker until you mentioned him to me, and I never heard of the town of Tucker until a few hours before I met you."

"You'd best go, then," she warned. "They're all over the country. Sheriff Eaton would take you in, but Wing wouldn't, nor any of his boys. They'll kill you on sight."

"Yeah," he agreed. "I can see that." Nevertheless, he didn't stir, but continued to roll a cigarette. She sat still, watching him curiously. Finally he looked up. "I'm in a fight," he admitted, "and not one I asked for. Cary is making this a mighty personal thing, ma'am, an' I reckon I ain't even figurin' on leavin'." He struck a match. "You got any chance of gettin' the ranch?"

"How could I? I have no money!"

"Supposin'," he suggested, squinting an eye against the smoke, "you had a pardner . . . with ten thousand dollars?"

Lisa shook her head. "Things like that don't happen," she said. "They just don't."

"I've got ten thousand dollars on me," Gatlin volunteered, "an' I've been pushed into this whether I like it or not. I say we ride into Tucker now an' we see this boss of yours, the lawyer. I figure he could get the deal all set up for us tomorrow. Are you game?"

"You . . . you really have that much?" She looked doubtfully at his shabby range clothes. "It's honest money?"

"I drove cattle to Montana," he said. "That was my piece of it. Let's go."

"Not so fast!" The words rapped out sharply. "I'll take that money, an' take it now! Woody, get the girl!"

For reply Jim slapped the spurs to the black and, at the same instant, slapped the sorrel a ringing blow. The horses sprang off together in a dead run. Behind them, a rifle shot rang out, and Jim felt the bullet clip past his skull. "Keep goin'!" he yelled. "Ride!"

At a dead run, they swung down the trail, and then Jim saw a side trail he had noticed on his left. He jerked his head at the girl and grabbed at her bridle. It was too dark to see the gesture, but she felt the tug and turned the sorrel after him, mounting swiftly up the steep side hill under the trees. There the soft needles made it impossible for their horses' hoofs to be heard, and Jim led the way, pushing on under the pines.

That it would be only a minute or so before

Cary discovered his error was certain, but each minute counted. A wall lifted on their right, and they rode on, keeping in the intense darkness close under it, but then another wall appeared on their left, and they were boxed in. Behind them they heard a yell, distant now, but indication enough their trail had been found. Boulders and slabs of rock loomed before them, but the black horse turned down a slight incline and worked his way around the rocks. From time to time, they spoke to each other to keep together, but he kept moving, knowing that Wing Cary would be close behind.

The cañon walls seemed to be drawing closer, and the boulders grew larger and larger. Somewhere Jim heard water running, and the night air was cool and slightly damp on his face. He could smell pine, so he knew that there were trees about and they had not ridden completely out of them. Yet Jim was becoming worried, for the cañon walls towered above them, and obviously there was no break. If this turned out to be a box cañon, they were bottled up. One man could hold this cañon corked with no trouble at all.

The black began to climb and in a few minutes walked out on a flat of grassy land. The moon was rising, but as yet there was no light in this deep cañon.

Lisa rode up beside him. "Jim"—it was the first time she had ever called him by name—"I'm afraid we're in for it now. Unless I'm mistaken, this is a box cañon. I've never been up here, but I've heard of it, and there's no way out."

"I was afraid of that." The black horse stopped as he spoke, and he heard water falling ahead. He urged the horse forward, but he refused to obey. Jim swung down into the darkness. "Pool," he said. "We'll find some place to hole up and wait for daylight."

They found a group of boulders and seated themselves among them, stripping the saddles from their horses and picketing them on a small patch of grass behind the boulders. Then, for a long time they talked the casual talk of two people finding out about each other. Jim talked of his early life on the Nueces, of his first trip into Mexico after horses when he was fourteen, and how they were attacked by Apaches. There had been three Indian fights that trip, two south of the border and one north of it.

He had no idea when sleep took him, but he awakened with a start to find the sky growing gray and to see Lisa Cochrane sleeping on the grass six feet away. She looked strangely young, with her face relaxed and her lips slightly parted. A dark tendril of hair had blown across her cheek. He turned away and walked out to the horses. The grass was thick and rich there.

He studied their position with care and found they were on a terrace separated from the end wall of the cañon only by the pool, at least an acre of clear, cold water into which a small fall poured from the cliff above. There were a few trees, and some of the scattered boulders they had encountered the previous night. The cañon on which they had come was a wild jumble of boulders and brush surmounted on either side by cliffs that lifted nearly three hundred feet. While escape might be impossible if Wing Cary attempted, as he surely would, to guard the opening, their own position was secure, too, for one man with a rifle might stand off an army from the terrace.

After he had watered the horses, he built a fire and put water on for coffee. Seeing some trout in the pool, he tried his luck, and from the enthusiasm with which they went for his bait, the pool could never have been fished before, or not in a long time.

Lisa came from behind the boulders just as the coffee came to a boil. "What is this? A picnic?" she asked brightly.

He grinned, touching his unshaven jaw. "With this beard?" He studied her a minute. "You'd never guess you'd spent the night on horseback or sleeping at the end of a cañon," he said. Then his eyes sobered. "Can you handle a rifle? I mean, well enough to stand off Cary's boys if they tried to come up here?"

She turned quickly and glanced down the

33

cañon. The nearest boulders to the terrace edge were sixty yards away, and the approach even that close would not be easy. "I think so," she said. "What are you thinking of?"

He gestured at the cliff. "I've been studyin' that. With a mite of luck, a man might make it up there."

Her face paled. "It isn't worth it. We're whipped, and we might as well admit it. All we can do now is sit still and wait until the ranch is sold."

"No," he said positively. "I'm goin' out of here if I have to blast my way out. They've made a personal matter out of this, now, and"— he glanced at her—"I sort of have a feeling you should have that ranch. Lookin' at it yesterday, I just couldn't imagine it without you. You lived there, didn't you?"

"Most of my life. My folks were friends of Uncle Dave's, and after they were killed, I stayed on with him."

"Did he leave you anything?" he asked.

She shook her head. "I . . . I think he expected me to marry Jim. . . . He always wanted it that way, but we never felt like that about each other, and yet Jim told me after Uncle Dave died that I was to consider the place my home, if he got it."

As they ate, he listened to her talk while he studied the cliff. It wasn't going to be easy, and yet it could be done.

A shout rang out from the rocks behind them, and they both moved to the boulders, but there was nobody in sight. A voice yelled again that Jim spotted as that of Wing Cary. He shouted a reply, and Wing yelled back: "We'll let Lisa come out if she wants, an' you, too, if you come with your hands up!"

Lisa shook her head, so Gatlin shouted back: "We like it here! Plenty of water, plenty of grub! If you want us, you'll have to come an' get us!"

In the silence that followed, Lisa said: "He can't stay, not if he attends the auction."

Jim turned swiftly. "Take the rifle. If they start to come, shoot an' shoot to kill. I'm going to take a chance."

Keeping out of sight behind the worn gray boulders, Gatlin worked his way swiftly along the edge of the pool toward the cliff face. As he felt his way along the rocky edge, he stared down into the water. That pool was deep, from the looks of it. And that was something to remember.

At the cliff face, he stared up. It looked even easier than he thought, and at one time and another he had climbed worse faces. However, once he was well up the face, he would be within sight of the watchers below—or would he?

III

He put a hand up and started working his way to a four-inch ledge that projected from the face of the rock and slanted sharply upward. There were occasional clumps of brush growing from the rock, and they would offer some security. A rifle shot rang out behind him, then a half dozen more, farther off. Lisa had fired at something and had been answered from down the cañon.

The ledge was steep, but there were good handholds, and he worked his way along it more swiftly than he would have believed possible. His clothing blended well with the rock, and by refraining from any sudden movements there was a chance that he could make it.

When almost two hundred feet up the face, he paused, resting on a narrow ledge, partly concealed by an outcropping. He looked up, but the wall was sheer. Beyond, there was a chimney, but almost too wide for climbing, and the walls looked slick as a blue clay side hill. Yet study the cliff as he would, he could see no other point where he might climb farther. Worse, part of that chimney was exposed to fire from below.

If they saw him, he was through. He'd be stuck, with no chance of evading their fire. Yet he knew he'd take the chance. Squatting on the ledge, he pulled off his boots, and, running a loop of pigging string through their loops, he slung them from his neck. Slipping thongs over his guns, he got into the chimney and braced his back against one side, then lifted his feet, first his left, then his right, against the opposite wall.

Whether Lisa was watching or not, he didn't know, but almost at that instant she began firing. The chimney was, at this point, all of six feet deep and wide enough to allow for climbing, but very risky climbing. His palms flat against the slippery wall, he began to inch himself upward, working his stocking feet up the opposite wall. Slowly, every movement a danger, his breath coming slowly, his eyes riveted on his feet, he began to work his way higher.

Sweat poured down his face and smarted in his eyes, and he could feel it trickling down his stomach under his wool shirt. Before he was halfway up, his breath was coming in great gasps, and his muscles were weary with the strain of opposing their strength against the walls to keep from falling. Then, miraculously, the chimney narrowed a little, and climbing was easier.

He glanced up. Not over twenty feet to go. His heart bounded, and he renewed his effort. A foot slipped, and he felt an agonizing moment when fear throttled him and he seemed about to fall. To fall meant to bound from that ledge and go down, down into that deep green pool at the foot of the cliff, a fall of nearly three hundred feet.

Something smacked against the wall near him and from below there was a shout. Then Lisa opened fire, desperately, he knew, to give him covering fire. Another shot splashed splinters in his face and he struggled wildly, sweat pouring from him, to get up those last few feet. Suddenly the rattle of fire ceased, and then opened up again. He risked a quick glance and saw Lisa Cochrane running out in the open, and, as she ran, she halted and fired.

She was risking her life, making her death or capture inevitable, to save him.

Suddenly a breath of air was against his cheek, and he hunched himself higher, his head reaching the top of the cliff. Another shot rang out and howled off the edge of the rock beside him. Then his hands were on the edge, and he rolled over onto solid ground, trembling in every limb.

There was no time to waste. He got to his feet, staggering, and stared around. He was on the very top of the mountain, and Tucker lay far away to the south. He seated himself and got his boots on, then slipped the thongs from his guns. Walking as swiftly as his still-trembling muscles would allow, he started south.

There was a creek, he remembered, that flowed down into the flatlands from somewhere near there, an intermittent stream, but with a cañon that offered an easy outlet to the plain below. Studying the terrain, he saw a break in the rocky plateau that might be it and started down the steep mountainside through the cedar, toward that break.

A horse was what he needed most. With a good horse under him, he might make it. He had a good lead, for they must come around the mountain, a good ten miles by the quickest trail. That ten miles might get him to town before they could catch him, to town and to the lawyer who would make the bid for them, even if Eaton had him in jail by that time. Suddenly, remembering how Lisa had run out into the open, risking her life to protect him, he realized he would willingly give his own to save her.

He stopped, mopping his face with a handkerchief. The cañon broke away before him, and he dropped into it, sliding and climbing to the bottom. When he reached the bottom, he started off toward the flat country at a swinging stride. A half hour later, his shirt dark with sweat, the cañon suddenly spread widely into the flat country. Dust hung in the air, and he slowed down, hearing voices.

"Give 'em a blow." It was a man's voice speaking. "Hear any more shootin'?"

"Not me." The second voice was thin and nasal. "Reckon it was my ears mistakin' themselves."

"Let's go, Eaton," another voice said. "It's too

hot here. I'm pinin' for some o' that good XY well water."

Gatlin pushed his way forward. "Hold it, Sheriff. You huntin' me?"

Sheriff Eaton was a tall, gray-haired man with a handlebar mustache and keen blue eyes. "If you're Gatlin, an' from the looks of you, you must be, I sure am. How come you're so all-fired anxious to get caught?"

Gatlin explained swiftly. "Lisa Cochrane's back there, an' they got her," he finished. "Sheriff, I'd be mighty pleased if you'd send a few men after her, or go yourself an' let the rest of them go to Tucker with me."

Eaton studied him. "What you want in Tucker?"

"To bid that ranch in for Lisa Cochrane," he said flatly. "Sheriff, that girl saved my bacon back there, an' I'm a grateful man. You get me to town to get that money in Lawyer Ashton's hands, an' I'll go to jail."

Eaton rolled his chaw in his lean jaws. "Dave Butler come over the Cut-Off with me, seen this ranch, then, an' would have it no other way but that he come back here to settle. I reckon I know what he wanted." He turned. "Doc, you'll git none of that XY water today. Take this man to Ashton, then put him in jail. An' make her fast."

Doc was a lean, saturnine man with a lantern jaw and cold eyes. He glanced at Gatlin, then nodded as he handed the reins of the extra horse they had brought to Gatlin. "If you say so, Sheriff. I sure was hopin' for some o' that good XY water, though. Come on, pardner."

They wheeled their horses and started for Tucker, Doc turning from the trail to cross the desert through a thick tangle of cedar and sagebrush. "Mite quicker this-away. Ain't nobody ever rides it, an' she's some rough."

It was high noon, and the sun was blazing. Doc led off, casting only an occasional glance back at Gatlin. Jim was puzzled, for the man made no show of guarding him. Was he deliberately offering him the chance to make a break? It looked it, but Jim wasn't having any. His one idea was to get to Tucker, see Ashton, and get his money down. They rode on, pushing through the dancing heat waves, no breeze stirring the air, and the sun turning the bowl into a baking oven.

Doc slowed the pace a little. "Hosses won't stand it," he commented, then glanced at Gatlin. "I reckon you're honest. You had a chance for a break an' didn't take it." He grinned wryly. "Not that you'd have got far. This here rifle o' mine sure shoots where I aim it at."

"I've nothin' to run from," Gatlin replied. "What I've said was true. My bein' in Tucker was strictly accidental."

The next half mile they rode side-by-side, entering now into a devil's playground of boulders and arroyos. Doc's hand went out, and Jim drew up. Buzzards roosted in a tree not far off the trail, a half dozen of the great birds. "Somethin' dead," Doc said. "Let's have a look."

Two hundred yards farther and they drew up. What had been a dappled gray horse lay in a saucer-like depression among the cedars. Buzzards lifted from it, flapping their great wings. Doc's eyes glinted, and he spat. "Jim Walker's mare," he said, "an' his saddle."

They pushed on, circling the dead horse.

Gatlin pointed. "Look," he said, "he wasn't killed. He was crawlin' away."

"Yeah"—Doc was grim—"but not far. Look at the blood he was losin'."

They got down from their horses, their faces grim. Both men knew what they'd find, and neither man was looking forward to the moment. Doc slid his rifle from the scabbard. "Jim Walker was by way o' bein' a friend o' mine," he said. "I take his goin' right hard."

The trail was easy. Twice the wounded man had obviously lain still for a long time. They found torn cloth where he had ripped up his shirt to bandage a wound. They walked on until they saw the gray rocks and the foot of the low bluff. It was a *cul-de-sac*.

"Wait a minute," Gatlin said. "Look at this." He indicated the tracks of a man who had walked up the trail. He had stopped there, and there was blood on the sage, spattered blood. The faces

42

of the men hardened, for the deeper impression of one foot, the way the step was taken, and the spattered blood told but one thing. The killer had walked up and kicked the wounded man.

They had little farther to go. The wounded man had nerve, and nothing had stopped him. He was backed up under a clump of brush that grew from the side of the bluff, and he lay on his face. That was an indication to these men that Walker had been conscious for some time, that he had sought a place where the buzzards couldn't get at him.

Doc turned, and his gray white eyes were icy. "Step your boot beside that track," he said, his rifle partly lifted.

Jim Gatlin stared back at the man and felt cold and empty inside. At that moment, familiar with danger as he was, he was glad he wasn't the killer. He stepped over to the tracks and made a print beside them. His boot was almost an inch shorter and of a different type.

"Didn't figger so," Doc said. "But I aimed to make sure."

"On the wall there," Gatlin said. "He scratched somethin'."

Both men bent over. It was plain, scratched with an edge of whitish rock on the slate of a small slab—**Cary done**—and no more.

Doc straightened. "He can wait a few hours more. Let's get to town."

. . .

Tucker's street was more crowded than usual when they rode up to Ashton's office and swung down. Jim Gatlin pulled open the door and stepped in. The tall, gray-haired man behind the desk looked up.

"You're Ashton?" Gatlin demanded. At the answering nod, he opened his shirt and unbuckled his money belt. "There's ten thousand there. Bid in the XY for Cochrane an' Gatlin."

Ashton's eyes sparkled with sudden satisfaction. "You're her partner?" he asked. "You're putting up the money? It's a fine thing you're doing, man."

"I'm a partner only in name. My gun backs the brand, that's all. She may need a gun behind her for a little while, an' I've got it."

He turned to Doc, but the man was gone. Briefly Gatlin explained what they had found and added: "Wing Cary's headed for town now."

"Headed for town?" Ashton's head jerked around. "He's here. Came in about twenty minutes ago."

Jim Gatlin spun on his heel and strode from the office. On the street, pulling his hat brim low against the glare, he stared left, then right. There were men on the street, but they were drifting inside now. There was no sign of the man called Doc or of Cary.

Gatlin's heels were sharp and hard on the

44

boardwalk. He moved swiftly, his hands swinging alongside his guns. His hard brown face was cool, and his lips were tight. At the Barrelhouse, he paused, put up his left hand, and stepped in. All faces turned toward him, but none was that of Cary.

"Seen Wing Cary?" he demanded. "He murdered Jim Walker."

Nobody replied, and then an oldish man turned his head and jerked it down the street. "He's gettin' his hair cut, right next to the livery barn. Waitin' for the auction to start up."

Gatlin stepped back through the door. A dark figure, hunched near the blacksmith shop, jerked back from sight. Jim hesitated, alert to danger, then quickly pushed on.

The red and white barber pole marked the frame building. Jim opened the door and stepped in. A sleeping man snored with his mouth open, his back to the street wall. The bald barber looked up, swallowed, and stepped back.

Wing Cary sat in the chair, his hair half trimmed, the white cloth draped around him. The opening door and sudden silence made him look up. "You, is it?" he said.

"It's me. We found Jim Walker. He marked your name, Cary, as his killer."

Cary's lips tightened, and suddenly a gun bellowed, and something slammed Jim Gatlin in the shoulder and spun him like a top, smashing him sidewise into the door. That first shot saved him from the second. Wing Cary had held a gun in his lap and fired through the white cloth. There was sneering triumph in his eyes, and, as though time stood still, Jim Gatlin saw the smoldering of the black-rimmed circles of the holes in the cloth.

He never remembered firing, but suddenly Cary's body jerked sharply, and Jim felt the gun buck in his hand. He fired again, and Wing's face twisted and his gun exploded into the floor, narrowly missing his own foot.

Wing started to get up, and Gatlin fired a third time, the shot nicking Wing's ear and smashing a shaving cup, spattering lather. The barber was on his knees in one corner, holding a chair in front of him. The sleeping man had dived through the window, glass and all.

Men came running, and Jim leaned back against the door. One of the men was Doc, and he saw Sheriff Eaton, and then Lisa tore them aside and ran to him. "Oh, you're hurt! You've been shot! You've . . . !"

His feet gave away slowly, and he slid down the door to the floor. Wing Cary still sat in the barbershop chair, his hair half clipped.

Doc stepped in and glanced at him, then at the barber. "You can't charge him for it, Tony. You never finished."

GAMBLE OF THE KT

For three days Shandy Gamble had been lying on his back in the Perigord House awaiting the stranger with the black mustache—Nichols, his name was—thinking if they were going to start cattle buying, they had better be moving. The season was already late.

Shandy Gamble was seventeen years old and tall for his age. In fact, he was tall for any age. Four inches over six feet, he was all feet, hands, and shoulders. With his shirt off you could count every rib in his lean body.

Perigord was the biggest town Shandy had ever seen. In fact, it was only the third town he had seen in his life. With the cattle buyers in town there was almost a thousand head of folks, and on the street Shandy felt uncomfortable and mighty crowded. Most of his time he spent down at the horse corrals or lying on his bed, waiting for Nichols.

He had come to town to buy himself a new saddle and bridle. Maybe a new hat and shirt. He was a saving man, Shandy Gamble was, despite his youth. Now he not only was holding his own money, but five hundred dollars belonging to

Nichols. Had it not been for that, he wouldn't have waited, for by now he was homesick for the KT outfit.

Nichols was a big powerful man with a smooth-shaved face and black, prominent eyes. He also had black hair and a black moustache.

Shandy had been leaning on the corral gate when Nichols had first approached him.

"Good afternoon, sir!" Nichols had thrust out a huge hand. "I understand you're a cattleman."

Shandy Gamble blinked. Nobody had ever called him a cattleman before and his chest swelled appreciably. He was a forty-dollar-a-month cowhand, although at the moment he did have five hundred and fifty-two dollars in his pocket.

Fifty-two dollars was saved from his wages, and the five hundred was half the reward money for nailing two horse thieves back in the cedar country. Shandy had tracked them back there for Deputy Sheriff Holloway, and when they killed Holloway, he got mad and went in after them. He brought one out dead and one so badly mauled he wished he was dead. There was a thousand dollars on their heads and Shandy tried to give it to Mrs. Holloway, but she would accept only half.

Thinking about Nichols now, Shandy shifted uneasily on the bed. It was time Nichols got back. The proposition had sounded good, no question about that.

"You can't beat it, Gamble," Nichols had said, "you know cattle and I've the connections in Kansas City and Chicago. We can ride over the country buying cattle, then ship and sell them. A nice profit for both of us."

"That would take money, and I ain't got much," Shandy had said.

Nichols eyed him thoughtfully. No use telling the boy he had seen that roll when Shandy paid for his room in advance.

"It won't take much to start"—Nichols scowled as he considered the size of Shandy's roll—"say a thousand dollars."

"Shucks," Shandy was regretful. "I ain't got but five hundred."

"Fine!" Nichols clapped him on the shoulder. "We're partners then! You put up five hundred and I'll put up five hundred! We'll bank that here and then start buying. I've got unlimited credit east of here, and when the thousand is gone, we'll draw on that. At this stage, you'll be the one doing most of the thinking, so you don't need to put as much cash into it as I do."

"Well . . ." Shandy had not been sure. It sounded like a good deal, and who knew cows better than he did? He had been practically raised with cows. "Maybe it would be a good deal," he said. "Old Ed France has a herd nobody's looked at . . . nice fat stock, too."

"Good!" Nichols clapped him on the shoulder

49

again. From his pocket, he took a long brown envelope and a sheaf of bills. Very carefully he counted off five hundred dollars and stuck it into the envelope. "Now your five hundred."

Shandy dug down and hauled out his bills and counted off the five hundred dollars and tucked it into the envelope.

"Now"—Nichols started to put the envelope in his pocket—"we'll go to the bank and . . ." He stopped, then withdrew the envelope. "No, you just keep this on you. We'll bank it later."

Shandy Gamble accepted the fat envelope and stuck it into his shirt.

Nichols glanced at his watch, then rubbed his jaw.

"Tell you what," Nichols said, "I've got to catch the stage for Holbrook. I'll be back tomorrow night. You stick around and, whatever you do, don't let this money out of your hands. I'll see you back at the hotel."

Shandy watched him go, shrugged, and went back to watching the horses. There was a fine black gelding there. If he was a cattle buyer, he would own that gelding, buy a new saddle and bridle, and some fancy clothes like Jim Finnegan wore, and would he show that outfit back on the KT!

Now, the wait for Nichols was dampening his enthusiasm for becoming a cattle buyer. Truth was, he liked the KT and liked working with the boys. They were a good outfit.

He rolled over on the bed and swung his feet to the floor. Reaching for his boots, he shoved his big feet into them and stood up.

To blazes with it! He'd open the envelope, leave the money in the bank for Nichols, and go back to the outfit. He was no cattle buyer, anyway. He was a cowhand.

Taking out the brown envelope, he ripped it open. Slowly he turned cold and empty inside, and stood there, his jaw slack, his shock of corn-silk hair hanging over his face. The envelope was stuffed with old newspaper pieces.

The spring grass faded from green to brown and dust gathered in the trails. Water holes shrank and the dried earth cracked around them and the cattle grew gaunt. It was a hard year on the caprock, and that meant work for the hands.

Shandy Gamble was in the saddle eighteen to twenty hours most days, rounding up strays and pushing them south to the gullies and remaining water holes. When he had returned from Perigord without his saddle, there was a lot of jawing about it, and the boys all had poked fun at Shandy, but he had grinned widely and taken it, letting them believe he had drunk it up or spent it on women.

Jim Finnegan rode out one day on a gray horse. He was looking the situation over and making estimates on the beef to be had after the fall roundup. Shandy was drifting south with three head of gaunted stock when they met. Gamble drew up and Finnegan joined him.

"Howdy, son. Stock looks poor."

"Yeah,"—Shandy dug for the makings—"we need rain plumb bad." He rolled his smoke, then asked quietly: "You ever hear of a buyer name of Nichols? Big, black-eyed man."

Shandy's description was accurate and painstaking, the sort of description a man might give who was used to reading signs and who thirty seconds after a glimpse of a horse or cow could describe its every hair and ailment.

"Nichols? You've forgotten the name, son. No, the *hombre* you describe is Abel Kotch. He's a card slick an' confidence man. Brute of a fighter, too. Brags he never saw the man could stand up to him in a fistfight."

"Seen him around?"

"Yeah, he was around Fort Worth earlier this year. He rousts around with the June boys."

The June boys. There were five of the Junes—the old man, Pete June, and the four outlaw sons, Alec, Tom, Buck, and Windy. All were gun slicks, badmen, dirty, unkempt drifters known to be killers, believed to be horse and cow thieves, and suspected of some out-and-out murders.

Two nights later, back at the bunkhouse, Johnny Smith rode in with the mail, riding down from Tuckup way where he had stopped to ask after some ironwork being done for the ranch by the Tuckup blacksmith. Tuckup was mostly an outlaw town, but the blacksmith there was the best around. Cowhands do most of their own work, but the man at Tuckup could make anything with iron and the KT boss had been getting some fancy andirons made for his fireplace.

"Killin' over to Tuckup," Johnny said as he swung down. "That Sullivan from Brady Cañon tangled with Windy June. Windy bored him plenty."

Shandy Gamble's head came up.

"June? The rest of that outfit there?" he asked.

"Sure, the whole shootin' match o' Junes!"

"Big, black-eyed fellow with 'em? Black mustache?"

"Kotch? Sure as you know he is. He whupped the blacksmith. Beat him so bad he couldn't finish the old man's andirons. That's a rough outfit."

The boss of the KT was talking to Jim Finnegan when Shandy strolled up.

"Boss, anything you want done over Tuckup way? I got to ride over there."

The boss glanced at him sharply. It was unlike Gamble to ask permission to go away from his work. He was a good hand, and worked like two men. If he wanted to go to Tuckup there was a reason.

"Yeah. Ask about my irons again. Too, you might have a look up around the water pocket. We're missin' some cows. If you find them, or see any suspicious tracks, come ahootin' an' we'll ride up that way."

Shandy Gamble was going to borrow a buckskin that belonged to the KT. He was a short-coupled horse with a wide head, good at cutting or roping, but a good trail horse, too.

Johnny Smith, who was mending a bridle, glanced up in time to see Gamble going out of the door with his rifle in his hand. That was not too unusual, with plenty of wolves and lions around, but Shandy was wearing two guns, something that hadn't happened for a long time. Johnny's brow puckered, then he shrugged and went back to work on the bridle.

The Tuckup Trail was a scar across the face of the desert. It was a gash in the plateau and everywhere was rock—red rock, pink rock, white, yellow, and buff rock—twisted and gnarled into weird shapes. By night it was a ghost land where a wide moon floated over the blasted remains of ancient mountains and by day it was an oven blazing with heat and dancing with dust devils and heat-waved distance.

Tuckup was a cluster of shabby, down-at-the-heel buildings tucked back into a hollow among the rocks. It boasted that there was a grave in

Boot Hill for every living person in town, and they always had two empty graves waiting to receive the next customers.

Tuckup was high, and despite the blazing heat of the day, a fire was usually welcome at night. The King High Saloon was the town's resort, meeting place, and hang-out. Second only to it was the stable, a rambling gloomy building full of stalls for sixty horses and a loft full of hay.

Shandy Gamble stabled his horse and gave it a good rubdown. It had a hard ride ahead of it, for he knew that there would be no remaining in town after he had done what he had to do.

Lean, gangling, and slightly stooped, he stood in the stable door and rolled a smoke. His shoulders seemed excessively broad above the narrow hips, and the two .44s hung with their butts wide and easy to his big hands. He wore jeans and a faded checked shirt. His hat was gray, dusty, and battered. There was a hole through the crown that one of the horse thieves he had chased had put there.

He studied the town. There was the saloon, a general store, the blacksmith shop, and livery stable. Beyond and around was a scattering of a dozen or so houses, mostly mere shacks. Then there were two bunkhouses that called themselves hotels.

Shandy Gamble walked slowly across to the

blacksmith shop. The smith was a burly man, and when he looked up, Shandy saw a deep, half-healed cut on his cheek bone and an eye still swollen and dark.

"KT irons ready?" Shandy asked, to identify himself.

"Will be." The smith stared at him. "Rider from there just here yestiddy. Your boss must be in a mighty hurry."

"Ain't that. I had some business over here. Know an *hombre* name of Kotch?"

The smith glared. "You bein' funny?"

"No. I got business with him."

"Trouble?"

"Uh-huh. I'm goin' to beat his head in."

The smith shrugged. "Try it if you want. I done tried, but not no more. He durned near kilt me."

"He won't kill me."

"Your funeral. He's up at the King High." The smith looked at him. "You be keerful. Them Junes is up there, too." He wiped his mustache. "KT, you better think again. You're only a kid."

"My feet make as big tracks as his'n."

"Goin' in, they may. Comin' out they may be a sight smaller."

Shandy Gamble's eyes were chill. "Like you said, it's my funeral."

He hitched his guns in place and started across the street. He was almost to the hitch rail in front of the King High when he saw a fresh hide hung over the fence. It was still bloody. Curiously, he walked back.

The brand had been cut away from the rest of the hide. Poking around in a pile of refuse ready for burning, he found it, scraped it clean, and tucked it into his pocket. He was turning when he looked up to see a man standing near him.

He was several inches shorter than Shandy, but he was wide and blocky. He wore his gun tied down and he looked mean. His cheeks were hollow and his eyes small.

"What you doin', pokin' around hyar?"

"Just lookin'." Shandy straightened to his full height. "Sort of proddin' around."

"Whar you from?"

"Ridin' for the KT."

The man's lips tightened. "Git out of hyar!"

"Don't aim to be in no hurry."

"You know who I am? I'm Tom June, an' when I say travel, I mean it!"

Shandy stood looking at him, his eyes mild.

"Well, now, Tom June, I've heard o' you. Heard you was a cow thief an' a rustler."

"Why you . . . !" His hand swept for his gun, but Shandy had no idea to start a shooting now. His long left slammed out, his fist balled and rock hard. It caught Tom June flush on the mouth as his hand swept back for his gun and his head came forward. At the same time, Shandy's right swung into the pit of the man's stomach and his left dropped to June's gun wrist.

The struggle was brief, desperate, and final. Shandy clubbed a big fist to the man's temple and he folded. Hurriedly, Shandy dragged him into a shed, disarmed and then tied him. The last job he did well. Then he straightened and walked back to the street.

A quick glance up and down, and then he went up the steps to the porch in front of the King High Saloon, and through the batwing doors.

Five men sat around a poker game. Shandy recognized the broad back instantly as that of Nichols, who he now knew was Abel Kotch. At least two of the others were Junes, as he could tell from their faces.

Shoving his hat back on his head, he stood behind Kotch and glanced down at his cards. Kotch had a good hand. The stack of money before him would come to at least two hundred dollars.

"Bet 'em," Shandy said.

Kotch stirred irritably in his chair.

"Shut up!" he said harshly.

Shandy's gun was in his hand, the muzzle against Kotch's ear.

"Bet 'em, I said, bet 'em strong."

Kotch's hands froze. The Junes looked up, staring at the gangling tow-headed youth.

"Beat it, kid!" one of the two Junes said sharply.

"You stay out of this, June!" Shandy Gamble's voice was even. "My argument's with this coyote. I'd as soon blow his head off as not, but iffen he does what he's told, the worst he'll get is a beatin'!"

Kotch shoved chips into the center of the table. The Junes looked at their cards and raised. Kotch bet them higher. He won. Carefully, he raked in the coin.

"This is Shandy Gamble, Kotch. You owe me five hundred. Count it out before I forget myself an' shoot you, anyway."

"There ain't five hundred here!" Kotch protested.

"There's better than four. Count it!"

"Well, what do you know, Windy?" The thin man grinned across the table. "Old Kotch run into the wrong *hombre* for once! Wish Buck was here to see this!"

Reluctantly, Kotch counted the money. It came to four hundred and ten dollars.

Coolly, Shandy Gamble pocketed the money. "All right," he said, "stand up mighty careful an' unload your pockets."

"What?" Kotch's face was red with fury. "I'll kill you for this!"

"Empty 'em. I want more money. I want a hundred an' twenty dollars more."

"You ain't got it comin'!" Kotch glared at him.

"Five hundred an' interest for one year at six

percent. You get it for me or I'll be forced to take your horse an' saddle."

"Why, you . . . !"

Shandy's gun lifted slightly and Abel Kotch shut up. His eyes searched the boy's face, and what he read there wasn't pleasant. Kotch decided suddenly that this youngster would shoot, and shoot fast.

Carefully, he opened his money belt and counted out the hundred and twenty dollars, which Gamble quietly stowed in his pocket. Then he holstered his gun and hitched the belts into place.

"Now, just for luck, Mister Cattle Buyer, I'm goin' to give you a lickin'!"

Kotch stared. "Why, you fool! You . . . !"

He saw the fist coming and charged, his weight slamming Shandy back against the wall, almost knocking the wind from him. Kotch jerked a knee up to Gamble's groin, but the boy had grown up in cow camps and cattle towns, cutting his fighting teeth on the bone-hard, rawhide-tough teamsters of the freight outfits. Gamble twisted and threw Kotch off balance, then hit him with a looping right that staggered the heavier man.

Kotch was no flash in the pan. He could fight and he knew it. He set himself, feinted, and then threw a hard right that caught the boy flush on the chin. Shandy staggered but recovered as

Kotch rushed, and, dropping his head, the boy butted the heavier man under the chin. Kotch staggered, swinging both hands. Straightening, Shandy walked into him, slugging.

They stood there, wide-legged, and slugged like madmen, their ponderous blows slamming and battering at head and body. Shandy's head sang with the power of those punches and his breath came in gasps, but he was lean and hard from years of work on the range, and he fell into a rhythm of punching. His huge fists smashed at the gambler like battering rams.

Turning, Gamble caught it on his leg, high up, but he managed to grab Kotch's boot, and jerked. Kotch's other foot lost the ground and he hit the floor hard. Gamble grabbed him by the shirt front and smashed him in the face, a free swing that flattened the bone in Kotch's nose. Then, jerking him erect, Shandy gripped him with his left hand and swung a looping blow to the wind. Kotch's knees buckled, and Shandy smashed him in the face again and again. Then he shoved him hard. Kotch staggered, brought up against the back wall and slid to a sitting position, his face bloody, his head loose on his neck.

Shandy Gamble drew back and hitched his belts into place again. He mopped his face with a handkerchief, while he got his breath back.

There were five men in the room, now, all enemies without doubt. Two of them were

Junes—obviously from earlier conversation they were Windy and Alec.

Shandy hitched his gun belts again and left his thumbs tucked in them. He looked at Windy June.

"Found a cowhide out back," he said casually, "carried a KT brand."

Instantly the room was still. Windy June was staring at him, his eyes ugly. Alec was standing with his right hand on the edge of the bar. The others spread suddenly, getting out of the way. This, then, was between himself and the Junes.

"What then?" Windy asked, low voiced.

"Your brother Tom didn't like it. I called him a rustler, and he didn't like that."

"You called Tom June a rustler?" Windy's voice was low with amazement. "And you're alive?"

"I took his gun away an' tied him up. I'm takin' him to the sheriff."

"You're takin' . . . why, you fool kid!"

"I'm takin' him, an', seein' as you Junes ride together, I reckon you an' Alec better come along, too."

Windy June was astonished. Never in his life had he been called like this, and here, in his own bailiwick, by a kid. But then he remembered the job this kid had done on Abel Kotch and his lips grew close and tight.

"You better git," he said, "while you're all in one piece!"

The bartender spoke: "Watch yourself, Windy. I know this kid. He's the one that brought the boys in from Cottonwood, one dead an' one almost."

Windy June smiled thinly.

"Look, kid. We don't want to kill you. There's two of us. If you get by us, there's still Buck an' Pop. You ain't got a chance with me alone, let alone the rest of them."

Shandy Gamble stood tall in the middle of the floor. His long face was sober.

"You better come along then, Windy, because I aim to take you in, dead or alive."

Windy June's hand was a blur of speed. Guns thundered and the walls echoed their thunder. In the close confines of the saloon a man screamed. There was the acrid smell of gunpowder as Shandy Gamble was weaving in the floor's middle, his guns stabbing flame. He fired, then moved forward. He saw Alec double over and sprawl across Windy's feet, his gun sliding across the floor.

Windy, like a weaving blade of steel, faced Shandy and fired. Gamble saw Windy June's body jerk with the slam of a .44, saw it jerk again, and twist, saw him going to his knees with blood gushing from his mouth, his eyes bitterly, wickedly alive, and the guns in his big fists hammering their futile bullets into the floor. Then Shandy fired again, and Windy June sprawled across Alec and lay still. In the moment of silence that followed the cannonading of the guns, Windy's foot twitched and his spur jingled.

Shandy Gamble faced the room, his eyes searching the faces of the other men.

"I don't want no trouble from you. Two of you load the bodies on their horses. I'm takin' 'em with me, like I said."

Abel Kotch sat on the floor, his shocked and bloody face stunned with amazement at the bodies that lay there. He had taken milk from a kitten and watched it turn into a raging mountain lion before his eyes. He sat very still. He was out of this. He wanted to stay out. He was going to make no move that could be misinterpreted.

Slowly, they took the bodies out and tied them on the horses of the two June boys. Shandy watched them, then walked across to the stable to get his own horse, his eyes alert for the other two Junes.

When he had the horses, he walked back to the shed and saw Tom June staring up at him.

"What happened? I heard shootin'."

"Yeah."

Shandy reached down and caught him by his jacket collar with his left hand and coolly dragged him out of the shed, his feet furrowing the ground. He took him to the front of the saloon and threw him bodily across his horse.

The bound man saw the two bodies, dripping

and bloody. He cried out, then began to swear, viciously and violently.

"Look out, kid."

Who spoke, he did not know, but Shandy Gamble glanced up and saw two other men who wore the brand of the June clan—Pop and Buck June, wide apart in the street. Their faces were set and ready.

Shandy Gamble stepped away from the horses into the street's center.

"You can drop your guns an' come with me!" he called.

Neither man spoke. They came on, steadily and inexorably. And then something else happened. Up the street behind them appeared a cavalcade of riders, and Shandy recognized his boss leading them. Beside him rode Johnny Smith and Jim Finnegan and behind them the riders from the KT.

"Drop 'em June!" The boss's voice rang out sharp and clear. "There's nine of us here. No use to die!"

The Junes stopped.

"No use, Buck," Pop June said, "the deck's stacked ag'in' us."

The KT boss rode on past and stopped. He stared at the dead Junes and the bound body of Tom. He looked at Shandy as if he had never seen him before.

"What got into you, Shandy?" he asked. "We'd

never have known, but Johnny told us when you heard the Junes were here you got your guns and left. Then Jim remembered you'd been askin' him about this here Kotch, who trailed with 'em."

Shandy shrugged, building a smoke. "Nothin'," he finally answered. "We'd had trouble, Kotch an' me."

He drew the patch of hide from his pocket. "Then there was this, out back. Tom started a ruction when he seen me find it."

Shandy Gamble swung into his saddle.

"I reckon the Junes'll talk, an' they'll tell you where the cows are. An', boss"—Shandy puckered his brow—"could I ride into Perigord? I want to get me a new saddle."

"You got the money?" The boss reached for his pocket.

"Yeah"—Shandy smiled—"I got it from Kotch. He'd been holdin' it for me."

"Holdin' it for him!" Finnegan exploded. "He trusted Kotch . . . with money?"

Kotch had come to the door and was staring out at them.

The boss chuckled. "Well, trust or not, looks like he collected."

SHOWDOWN TRAIL

I

Everything was quiet in Mustang. Three whole days had passed without a killing. The townsfolk, knowing their community, were not fooled, but rather had long since resigned themselves to the inevitable and would, in fact, be relieved when the situation was back to normal with a killing every day, or more on hot days. When there had been no killing for several days, pressure mounted because no one knew who would be next. Moreover, with Clay Allison, who had killed thirty men, playing poker over at the Morrison House, and Black Jack Ketchum, who richly deserved the hanging he was soon to get, sleeping off a drunk at the St. James, trouble could be expected.

The walk before the St. James was cool at this hour, and Captain Tom Kedrick, a stranger in town, sat in a well-polished chair and studied the street with interested eyes. He was a tall young man with rusty brown hair and green eyes, quiet-mannered and quick to smile. Women never failed to look twice, and, when their eyes met his, their hearts pounded, a fact of which Tom Kedrick was totally unaware. He knew women seemed to like him, but it never failed to leave him mildly astonished when they liked him very much, which they often did.

The street he watched was crowded with buckboards, freight wagons, a newly arrived stage and one about to depart. All the hitch rails were lined with saddled horses wearing a variety of brands. Kedrick was suddenly aware that a young man stood beside him, and he glanced up. The fellow was scarcely more than a boy and he had soft brown eyes and hair that needed cutting.

"Cap'n Kedrick?" he inquired. "John Gunter sent me. I'm Dornie Shaw."

"Oh, yes!" Kedrick got to his feet, smiling, and thrust out his hand. "Nice to know you, Shaw. Are you working for Gunter?"

Shaw's soft brown eyes were faintly ironic. "With him," he corrected. "I work for no man."

"I see."

Kedrick did not see at all, but he was prepared to wait and find out. There was something oddly disturbing about this young man, something that had Kedrick on edge and queerly alert. "Where's Gunter now?"

"Down the street. He asked me to check an' see if you were here, an', if you were, to ask you to stick around close to the hotel. He'll be along soon."

"All right. Sit down, why don't you?"

Shaw glanced briefly at the chairs. "I'll stand. I never sit in no chair with arms on them. Apt to get in the way."

"In the way?" Kedrick glanced up, and then his eyes fell to the two guns Shaw wore, their butts hanging wide. "Oh, yes! I see." He nodded at the guns. "The town marshal doesn't object?"

Dornie Shaw looked at him, smiling slowly. "Not to me, he don't. Wouldn't do him no good if he did." He added after a minute: "Anyway, not in Mustang. Too many hardcases. I never seen a marshal could make it stick in this town."

Kedrick smiled. "Hickok? Earp? Masterson?"

"Maybe"—Dornie Shaw was openly skeptical—"but I doubt it. Allison's here. So's Ketchum. Billy the Kid's been around, and some of that crowd. A marshal in this town would have to be mighty fast, an' prove it ever' day."

"Maybe you're right." He studied Shaw surreptitiously. What was it about him that was so disturbing? Not the two guns, for he had seen many men who wore guns, had been reared among them, in fact. No, it was something else, some quality he could not define, but it was a sort of lurking menace, an odd feeling with such a calm-eyed young man.

"We've got some good men," Shaw volunteered, after a minute. "Picked up a couple today. Laredo Shad's goin' to be one of the best, I'm thinkin'. He's a tough hand, an' gun-wise as all get out. Three more come in today. Fessenden, Poinsett, an' Goff."

Obviously, from the manner in which he spoke, the names meant much to Shaw, but they meant exactly nothing to Kedrick. Fessenden seemed to strike some sort of a responsive note but he could not put a finger on it. His eyes strayed down the street, studying the crowd. "You think they'll really fight?" he asked. "Are there enough of them?"

"That bunch?" Shaw's voice was dry. "They'll fight, all right. You got some tough boys in that outfit. Injun scrappers, an' such like. They won't scare worth a damn." He glanced curiously at Kedrick. "Gunter says you're a fighter."

Was that doubt in Shaw's voice? Kedrick smiled, then shrugged. "I get along. I was in the Army, if that means anything."

"Been West before?"

"Sure! I was born in California, just before the rush. When the war broke out, I was sixteen, but I went in with a bunch from Nevada. Stayed in a couple of years after the war, fighting Apaches."

Shaw nodded, as if satisfied. "Gunter thinks well of you, but he's the only one of them, an' not the most important one."

A short, thick-set man with a square-cut beard looking enough like General Grant to be his twin was pushing through the crowd toward

70

them. He even smoked a thick, black cigar. The man walking beside him was as tall as Kedrick, who stood an easy inch above six feet. He had a sharply cut face and his eyes were cold, but they were the eyes of a man born to command, a man who could be utterly ruthless. That would be Colonel Loren Keith. That meant there was one yet, who he must meet. The man Burwick. The three were partners, and of the three only Burwick was from the area.

Gunter smiled quickly, his lips parting over clenched white teeth that gripped his cigar. He thrust out his hand. "Good to see you, Kedrick! Colonel, this is our man! If there ever was a man born to ramrod this thing through, this is the one. I told you of that drive he made for Patterson. Took those cattle through without losing a head, rustlers an' Comanches be damned."

Keith nodded, his cold eyes taking in Kedrick at a glance. "Captain . . . that was an Army title, Kedrick?"

"Army. The Civil War."

"I see. There was a Thomas Kedrick who was a sergeant in the fighting against the Apaches."

"That was me. All of us went down some in rank after the troops were discharged."

"How much time in the war?" Keith's eyes still studied him.

"Four years, and two campaigning in the Southwest."

"Not bad. You should know what to expect in a fight." His eyes went to Kedrick's, faintly supercilious. "I have twelve years, myself. Regular Army."

Kedrick found that Keith's attitude irritated him. He had meant to say nothing about it, but suddenly he was speaking. "My American Army experience, Colonel, was only part of mine. I was with Bazaine, at the defense of Metz, in the Franco-Prussian War. I escaped, and was with MacMahon at the Battle of Sedan."

Keith's eyes sharpened and his lips thinned. Kedrick could feel the sharp dislike rising in the man. Keith was defiantly possessed of a strong superiority complex.

"Is that all?" he asked coolly.

"Why, no. Since you ask, it was not. I was with Wolseley, in the Second Ashanti War in Africa. And I was in the two-year campaign against the Tungans of northern T'ien Shan . . . with the rank of general."

"You seem to get around a good bit," Keith said dryly, "a genuine mercenary."

Kedrick smiled, undisturbed. "If you like. That's what you want here, isn't it? Men who can fight? Isn't it customary for some men to hire others to do their fighting for them?"

Colonel Keith's face flamed, then went white, but before he could speak, a big, square-faced man thrust himself through the crowd and

72

stopped to face them. "You, is it, Gunter? Well, I've heard tell the reason why you're here, an', if you expect to take from hard-workin' men the land they've slaved for, you better come a-shootin'!"

Before anyone could speak, Dornie slid between Keith and Gunter and fronted the man. "You lookin' for trouble? You want to start your shootin' now?"

His voice was low, almost a purr, but Kedrick was startled by the shocked expression on the man's face. He drew back, holding his hands wide. "I wasn't bracin' you, Dornie. Didn't even know you was around."

"Then get out!" Shaw snarled, passion suddenly breaking through his calmness, and something else, something Kedrick spotted with a shock— the driving urge to kill!

"Get out!" Shaw repeated. "An' if you want to live, keep goin'!"

Stumblingly the man turned and ducked into the hastily assembled crowd, and Tom Kedrick, scanning their faces, found hard indifference there, or hatred. In no face did he see warmth or friendly feeling. He frowned thoughtfully, then turned away.

Gunter caught his arm, eager to take advantage of the break the interruption had made to bring peace between the two. "You see what we're up against?" he began. "Now that was Peters. He's harmless, but there's others would have drawn, and drawn fast. They won't be all like that. Let's go meet Burwick."

Kedrick fell in beside Gunter who carefully interposed himself between the two men. Once, Tom glanced back. What had become of Dornie Shaw he did not know, but he did know his second in command, which job was Shaw's, was a killer. He knew the type from of old.

Yet he was disturbed more than he cared to admit by the man who had braced them. Peters had the look of an honest man, even if not an intelligent one. Of course, there might be honest men among them, if they were men of Peters's stripe. He was always a follower, and he might follow where the wrong men led. Certainly, if this land was going to Gunter, Keith, and Burwick through a government bill, there could be nothing wrong with it. If the government sold the land to them, squatters had no rights there. Still, if there were many like Peters, the job was not going to be all he had expected.

Gunter stopped before a square, stone house set back from the street. "This here's headquarters," he said. "We hole up here when in town. Come on in."

A wide verandah skirted the house, and, as they stepped upon it, they saw a girl in a gray skirt and white blouse sitting a few feet away with an open book in her lap.

Gunter halted. "Colonel, you've met Miss Duane."

"Cap'n Kedrick, my niece, Consuelo Duane."

Their eyes met—and held. For a breathless moment, no voice was lifted. Tom Kedrick felt as though his muscles had gone dead, for he could not move. Her own eyes were wide, startled.

Kedrick recovered himself with a start. He bowed. "Miss Duane!"

"Captain Kedrick"—somehow she was on her feet and moving toward him—"I hope you'll like it here!"

His eyes had not left hers, and now color was coming into her cheeks. "I shall," he said gently. "Nothing can prevent me now."

"Don't be too sure of that, Captain." Keith's voice was sharp and cold. "We are late for our visit. Let's be going. Your pardon, Connie. Burwick is waiting."

Kedrick glanced back as he went through the door, and the girl was still standing there, poised, motionless.

Keith's irritation was obvious, but Gunter seemed to have noticed nothing. Dornie Shaw, who had materialized from somewhere, glanced briefly at Kedrick, but said nothing at all. Coolly he began to roll a smoke.

II

Burwick crouched behind a table. He was an incredibly fat man, and incredibly dirty. A stubble of graying beard covered his jowls and his several chins, yet the eyes that measured Kedrick from beneath the almost hairless brows were sharp, malignant, and set close alongside a nose too small for his face. His shirt was open, and the edge of the collar was greasy. Rims of black marked each fingernail.

He glanced at the others, then back at Kedrick. "Sit down!" he said. "You're late! Business won't wait!" His bulbous head swung from Kedrick to Gunter. "John, this the man who'll ramrod those skunks off that land? This him?"

"Yes, that's Kedrick," Gunter said hastily. Oddly enough, he seemed almost frightened of Burwick. Keith had said nothing since they entered the room. Quietly he seemed to have withdrawn, stepped momentarily from the picture. It was, Kedrick was to discover, a faculty he had when Burwick was near. "He'll do the job, all right."

Burwick turned his eyes on Kedrick after a moment and nodded. "Know a good deal about you, son." His voice was almost genial. "You'll do, if you don't get too soft with them. We've no time to waste, you understand. They've had notice to move. Give 'em one more notice, then get 'em off or bury 'em! That's your business, not mine. I'll ask the questions," he added sharply, "an' I'll see nobody else does. What happens here is our business."

He dismissed Kedrick from his mind and turned his attention to Gunter. "You've ordered like I told you? Grub for fifty men for fifty days? Once this situation is cleaned up, I want to get started at once. The sooner we have work started, the sooner we'll be all set. I want no backfiring on this job."

Burwick turned sharply to Tom Kedrick. "Ten days! I give you ten days! If you need more than five, I'll be disappointed. If you've not the heart for it, turn Dornie loose. Dornie'll show 'em." He cackled suddenly. "That's right! Dornie'll show 'em!" He sobered down, glanced at the papers on his desk, then without looking up: "Kedrick, you can go. Dornie, you run along, too."

Kedrick hesitated, then arose. "How many of these men are there?" he asked suddenly. "Have any of them families?"

Gunter turned on him nervously. "I'll tell you all you need to know, Tom. See you later."

Kedrick shrugged and, picking up his hat, walked out. Dornie Shaw had already vanished. Yet when he reached the verandah, Connie Duane still sat there, only now she was not reading, merely staring over the top of her book at the dusty, sun-swept street.

He paused, hat in hand. "Have you been in Mustang long?"

She looked up, studying him for a long minute before she spoke. "Why, no. Not long. Yet long enough to learn to love and hate." She turned her eyes to the hills, then back to him. "I love this country, Captain, can you understand that? I'm a city girl, born and bred in the city, and yet when I first saw those red rock walls, those lonely mesas, the desert, the Indian ponies . . . why, Captain, I fell in love! This is my country! I could stay here forever!"

Surprised, he studied her again, more pleased than he could easily have admitted. "That's the way I feel about it. But you said to love and to hate. You love the country. Now what do you hate?"

"Some of the men who infest it, Captain. Some of the human wolves it breeds, and others, bred somewhere, who come to it to feed off the ones who came earlier and were more courageous but are less knowing, less tricky."

More and more surprised, he leaned on the rail. "I don't know if I follow you, Miss Duane. I haven't been here long, but I haven't met any of those you speak of."

She looked up at him, her eyes frank and cool. Slowly she closed her book, stood up, and turned toward the door. "You haven't, Captain?" Her voice was suddenly cool. "Are you sure? At this moment, I am wondering if you are not one of them." She stepped through the door and was gone.

Tom Kedrick stood for a moment, staring after her. When he turned away, it was with a puzzled frown on his face. Now what did she mean by that? What did she know about him that could incline her to such a view? Despite himself, he was both irritated and disturbed. Coupled with the anger of the man Peters, it offered a new element to his thinking. Yet, how could Consuelo Duane, John Gunter's niece, have the same opinions owned by Peters? No doubt they stemmed from different sources.

Troubled, he walked on down to the street of the town and stood there, looking around. He had not yet changed into Western clothes, and still wore his flat-crowned, flat-brimmed black hat, which he would retain, and a tailored gray suit with black Western-style boots. Pausing on the corner, he slowly rolled a cigarette and lighted it. He made a dashing, handsome figure as he stood there in his perfectly fitted suit, his lean, bronzed face strong, intelligent, and interesting. Both men and women glanced at him, and most of them twice. His military erectness, broad shoulders, and cool self-possession were enough to mark him in any crowd. His mind had escaped his immediate problem now and was lost in the never-ending excitement of a crowded Western street. All jammed together without rhyme or reason, such places held all types and manner of men.

For the West was of all things a melting pot. Adventurers came to seek gold, new lands, excitement. Gamblers, women of the oldest and most active profession, thugs, gunmen, cow rustlers, horse thieves, miners, cowhands, freighters, and just drifters, all crowded the street. That bearded man in the sun-faded red wool shirt might, if prompted, start to spout Shakespeare. The slender young man talking to the girl in the buckboard might have graduated from Oxford, and the white-faced gambler might be the scion of an old Southern family.

There was no knowing in this strangest, most exciting, and colorful of countries, during its most exciting time. All classes, types, and nationalities had come West, all looking for the pot of gold at the foot of any available rainbow, and most of them were more engrossed in the looking than the finding. All men wore guns, most of them in plain sight. Few of them would hesitate to use them if need be. The man who fought with his fists was a rarity, although present.

A big man lurched from the crowd. Tom glanced at him, and their eyes met. Obviously the man had been drinking and was hunting trouble, and, as their eyes met, he stopped. Sensing trouble, other passers-by stopped, too.

"So?" The big man stood, wide-legged, his sleeves rolled above thick, hairy forearms. " 'Nother one of them durn' thieves. Land stealers!" He chuckled suddenly. "Well, your murderer ain't with you now to save your bacon, an' I aim to git my share of you right now. Reach!"

Kedrick's mouth was dry, but his eyes were calm. He held the cigarette in his right hand near his mouth. "Sorry, friend, I'm not packing a gun. If I were, I'd still not kill you. You're mistaken, man, about that land. My people have a rightful claim to it."

"Have they, now?" The big man came a step nearer, his hand on the butt of his gun. "The right to take from a man the land he's sweated over? To tear down his home? To run his kids out on the desert?"

Despite the fact that the man was drunk, Tom Kedrick saw beyond it a sullen and honest fury—and fear. Not fear of him, for this man was not afraid, nor would he be afraid of even Dornie Shaw. He was afraid for his family. The realization of that fact struck Kedrick and disturbed him anew. More and more he was questioning the course he had chosen.

The crowd murmured and was ugly. Obviously their sympathies were with the big man, and against Kedrick. A low murmur, then a rustling in the crowd, and suddenly, deathly silence. Kedrick saw the big man's face pale and heard someone whisper hoarsely: "Look out, Burt. It's Dornie Shaw."

Kedrick was suddenly aware that Shaw had moved up beside him. "Let me have him, Cap'n." Shaw's voice was low. "It's time this here was stopped."

Kedrick's voice was sharp, cold. "No! Move back, Shaw! I'll fight my own battles!"

"But you ain't got a gun!" Shaw's voice was sharper in protest.

Burt showed no desire to retreat. That the appearance of Shaw was a shock was evident, but this man was not Peters. He was going to stand his ground. His eyes, wary now but puzzled, shifted from Shaw to Kedrick, and Tom took an easy step forward, putting him almost within arm's length of Burt.

"Shaw's not in this, Burt," he said quietly. "I've no quarrel with you, man, but no man calls me without getting his chance. If you want what I've got, don't let the fact that I'm not armed stop you. I wanted no quarrel, but you do, so have at it!"

Suspicion was in the big man's eyes. He had seen guns come from nowhere before, and especially from men dressed as this one did. He was not prepared to believe that Kedrick would face him unarmed. "You got a gun!" he snapped. "You got a hide-out, you damned coyote!"

He jerked his gun from the holster and in that instant Tom Kedrick moved. The edge of his left hand chopped down on the rising wrist of the gun hand, and he stepped in, whipping up his right in an uppercut that packed all the power in his lean, whipcord body. The punch was fast and perfectly timed, and the crack of it on the corner of Burt's jaw was like the crack of a teamster's whip. Burt hit the walk just one split second after his gun, and hit it right on his shoulder blades.

Coolly then, Kedrick stooped and picked up the gun, an old 1851 Model Navy revolver. He stood over the man, his eyes searching the crowd. Wherever he looked, there were hard, blank faces. He glanced down at Burt, and the big man was slowly sitting up, shaking his big head. He darted to lift his right hand and gave a sudden gasp of pain. He stared at it, then looked up. "You broke my wrist!" he said. "It's busted! An' me with my plowin' to do!"

"Better get up," Kedrick said quietly. "You asked for it, you know." When the man was on his feet, Kedrick calmly handed him his six-shooter. Their eyes met over the gun and Kedrick smiled. "Take it. Drop it down in your holster an' forget it. I'm not worried. You're not the man to shoot another in the back."

Calmly he turned his back and walked slowly

83

away down the street. Before the St. James he paused. His fingers trembled ever so slightly as he took out a paper and shook tobacco into it.

"That was slick." It was Dornie Shaw's soft voice. His brown eyes probed Kendrick's face curiously. "Never seen the like. Just slapped his wrist and busted it."

With Keith, John Gunter had come up, smiling broadly. "Saw it all, son. That'll do more good than a dozen killings. Just like Tom Smith used to do. Old Bear Creek Tom who handled some of the toughest rannies that ever came over the trail with nothin' but his fists."

"What would you have done if he had jerked that gun back and fired?" Keith asked.

Kedrick shrugged, wanting to forget it. "He hadn't time," he said quietly, "but there are answers to that, too."

"Some of the boys will be up to see you tonight, Tom," Gunter advised. "I've had Dornie notify Shad, Fessenden, and some of the others. Better figure on a ride out there tomorrow. Makin' a start, anyway. Just sort of ride around with some of the boys to let 'em know we ain't foolin'."

Kedrick nodded, and after a brief discussion went inside and to his room. Certainly, he reflected, the West had not changed. Things still happened fast out here.

He pulled off his coat, waistcoat, and vest, then

his boots. Stripped to the waist, he sat down on the bed and dug into his valise. For a couple of minutes he dug around and then drew out two well-oiled holsters and gun belts. In the holsters were two .44 Russian pistols, a Smith & Wesson gun, manufactured on order for the Russian Army, and one of the most accurate shooting pistols on the market. Carefully he checked the loads, then returned the guns to their holsters and put them aside. Digging around again, he drew out a second pair of guns, holsters, and belts. Each of these was a Walch twelve-shot Navy pistol, caliber .36, and almost identical in size and weight to the Frontier Colt or the .44 Russian. Rarely seen in the West, and disliked by some, Kedrick had used the guns on many occasions and found them always satisfactory. There were times when the added firepower was a big help. As for stopping power, the .36 in the hands of a good marksman lacked but little offered by the heavier .44 caliber.

Yet, there was a time and a place for everything, and these guns had an added tactical value. Carefully he wrapped them once more and returned them to the bottom of his valise. Then he belted on the .44 Russians and, digging out his Winchester, carefully cleaned, oiled, and loaded it. Then he sat down on the bed and was about to remove his guns again and stretch out, when there was a light tap at the door.

"Come in," said Kedrick, "and, if you're an enemy, I'll be pleased to know you."

The door opened and closed all in a breath. The man that stood with his back to it, facing Kedrick, was scarcely five feet four, yet almost as broad as he was tall, but all of it sheer power of bone and muscle and not an ounce of fat anywhere. His broad, brown face might have been carved from stone, and the bristle of short-cropped hair above it was black as a crow's wing. The man's neck spread to broad, thick shoulders. On his right hip he packed a gun. In his hand he held a narrow-brimmed hard hat.

Kedrick leaped to his feet. "Dai!" The name was an explosion of sound. "Dai Reid! And what are you doing in this country?"

"Ah? So it's that you ask, is it? Well, it's trouble there is, much of trouble! An' you that's by way of bringin' it!"

"Me?" Kedrick waved to a chair. "Tell me what you mean."

The Welshman searched his face, then seated himself, his huge palms resting on his knees. His legs were thick-muscled and bowed. "It's the man Burwick you're with? An' you've the job taken to run us off the land? There changed you are, Tom, an' for the worse."

"You're one of them? You're on the land Burwick, Keith, and Gunter claim?"

"I am that. And a sight of work I've done on it,

too. An' now the rascals would be puttin' me off. Well, they'll have a fight to move me, an' you, too, if you're to stay one of them."

Kedrick studied the Welshman thoughtfully. All his doubts had come to a head now, for this man he knew. His own father had been Welsh, his mother Irish, and Dai Reid had been friend to them both. Dai had come from the old country with his father, had worked beside him when he courted his mother, and, although much younger than Gwilym Kedrick, he had come West with him, too.

"Dai," he said slowly, "I'll admit that today I've been having doubts of all this. You see, I knew John Gunter after the war, and I took a herd of cattle over the trail for a friend of his. There was trouble that year, the Indians holding every herd and demanding large numbers of cattle for themselves, the rustlers trying to steal whole herds, and others demanding money for passage across land they claimed. I took my herd through without paying anything but a few fat beefs for the Indians, who richly deserved them. But not what they demanded . . . they got what I wanted to give. Gunter remembered me from that and knew something of my war record, so when he approached me in New Orleans, his proposition sounded good. And this is what he told me.

"His firm . . . Burwick, Keith, and Gunter . . . had filed application for the survey and purchase

87

of all or parts of nearly three hundred sections of land. They made oath that this land was swampland or overflowed and came under the General Land Office ruling that it was land too wet for irrigation at seeding time, though later requiring irrigation, and therefore subject to sale as swamp. He went on to say that they had arranged to buy the land, but that a bunch of squatters were on it who refused to leave. He wanted to hire me to lead a force to see the land was cleared, and he said that as most of them were rustlers, outlaws, or renegades of one sort or another, there would be fighting and force would be necessary."

Dai nodded. "Right he was as to the fighting, but renegades, no. Well,"—he smiled grimly past his pipe—"I'd not be saying that now, but there's mighty few. There are bad apples in all barrels, one or two, but most of us be good people, with homes built and crops in. An' did he tell you that their oath was given that the land was unoccupied? Well, given it was! And let me tell you. Ninety-four sections have homes on them, some mighty poor, but homes. Shrewd they were with the planning. Six months the notices must be posted, but they posted them in fine print and where few men could read, and three months are by before anything is noticed, and by accident only. So now they come to force us off, to be sure the land is unoccupied and ready. As for swamp, 'tis desert now, and always desert. Crops can only be grown where the water is, an' little enough of that." Dai shook his head and knocked out his short-stemmed pipe. "Money we've none to fight them, no lawyers among us, although one who's as likely to help, a newspaper man, he is. But what good without money to send him to Washington?" The Welshman's face was gloomy. "They'll beat us, that we know. They've money to fight us with, and tough men, but some of them will die on the ground and pay for it with their red blood, and those among us there are who plan to see 'tis not only the hired gunners who die, but the high an' mighty. You, too, lad, if among them you stay."

Kedrick was thoughtful. "Dai, this story is different from the one I've had. I'll have to think about it, and tomorrow we ride out to look the land over and show ourselves."

Reid looked up sharply. "Don't you be one of them! We've plans made to see no man gets off alive if we can help it."

"Look, man." Kedrick leaned forward. "You've got to change that. I mean, for now. Tomorrow it's mainly a show of force, a threat. There will be no shooting, I promise you. We'll ride out, look around, then ride back. If there's shooting, your men will start it. Now you go back to them and stop it. Let them hold off, and let me look around."

89

Dai Reid got slowly to his feet. "Ah, lad, 'tis good to see you again, but under happier circumstances I wish it were! I'd like to have you to the house for supper and a game, as in the old days. You'd like the wife I have."

"You? Married?" Kedrick was incredulous. "I'd never believe it!"

Dai grinned sheepishly. "Married it is, all right, and happy, Tom." His face darkened. "Happy if I can keep my ground. But one promise I make. If your bloody riders take my ground, my body will be there where they ride past, and it will be not alone, but with dead men around."

Long after the Welshman had gone, Tom Kedrick sat silently and studied the street beyond the window. Was this what Consuelo Duane had meant? Whose side was she on? First, he must ride over the land, see it for himself, and then he must have another talk with Gunter. Uneasily he looked again at the faces of the men in his mind. The cold, wolf-like face of Keith, the fat, slobby face of Burwick, underlined with harsh, domineering power, and the face of Gunter, friendly, affable, but was it not a little—sly?

From outside came the noise of a tinny piano and a strident female voice singing. Chips rattled, and there was the constant rustle of movement and of booted feet. Somewhere a spur jingled, and Tom Kedrick got to his feet and slipped into a shirt. When he was dressed again, with his guns belted on, he left his room and walked down the hall to the lobby.

From a room beside his, a man stepped and stared after him. It was Dornie Shaw.

III

Only the dweller in the deserts can know such mornings, such silences, drowsy with warmth and the song of the cicadas; nowhere but in the desert shall the far miles stand out so clearly, the mesas, towers, and cliffs so boldly outlined. Nowhere will the cloud shadows island themselves as on the desert, offering their brief respite from the sun.

Six riders, their saddles creaking, six hard men, each lost in the twisted arroyos of his own thoughts, were emerging upon the broad desert. They were men who had used their guns to kill and would use them so again. Some of them were already doomed by the relentless and ruthless tide of events, and to the others their time, too, would come. Each of them was alone, as men who live by the gun are always alone, each man a potential enemy, each shadow a danger. They rode jealously, their gestures marked by restraint, their eyes by watchfulness.

A horse blew through his nostrils, a hoof clicked on a stone, someone shifted in his saddle and sighed. These were the only sounds. Tom Kedrick rode an Appaloosa gelding, fifteen hands even, with iron-gray forequarters and starkly white hindquarters splashed with tear-shaped spots of solid black—a clean-limbed horse, strong and fast, with quick, intelligent eyes and interested ears.

When they had bunched to start their ride, Laredo Shad had stopped to stare at the horse, walking around it admiringly. "You're lucky, friend. That's a horse! Where'd you find him?"

"Navajo remuda. He's a Nez Perce war horse, a long ways off his reservation."

Kedrick had noticed the men as they gathered and how they all sized him up carefully, noting his Western garb, and especially the low-hung, tied-down guns. They had seen him yesterday, in the store clothes he had worn from New Orleans, but now they could size him up better, judge him with their own kind.

He was tall and straight, and of his yesterday's clothing only the black, flat-crowned hat remained, the hat and the high-heeled rider's boots. He wore a gray wool shirt now and a black silk kerchief around his neck. His jeans were black, and the two guns rode easily in position, ready for the swing of his hand.

Kedrick had seen them bunch, and, while they all were there, he had said simply: "All right, let's go!"

They had mounted up. Kedrick had noted slender, wiry Dornie Shaw, the great bulk of Si Fessenden, lean, bitter Poinsett, the square, blond Lee Goff, sour-faced Clauson, the oldest of the lot, and the lean Texan, Laredo Shad. Moving out, he had glanced at them. Whatever else they might be, they were fighting men. Several times Shaw had glanced at his guns.

"You ain't wearin' Colts?"

"No, Forty-Four Russians. They are a good gun, one of the most accurate ever built." He had indicated the trail ahead with a nod. "You've been out this way before?"

"Yeah, we got quite a ride. We'll noon at a spring I know just over the North Fork. There's some deep cañons to cross, then a big peak. The Indians an' Spanish called it The Orphan. All wild country. Right behind there we'll begin strikin' a few of 'em." He grinned a little, showing his white, even teeth. "They are scattered all over hell's half acre."

"Dornie," Goff had asked suddenly, "you figure on ridin' over to the *malpais* this trip?"

Clauson had chuckled. "Sure, he will! He should've give up long ago, but he's sure hard to whip! That girl has set her sights higher'n any west-country gunslinger."

"She's shapely, at that!" Goff was openly admiring. "Right shapely, but playin' no fav'rites."

"Maybe they're playin' each other for what

they can git," Poinsett had said wryly. "Maybe that's where he gets all the news he's tellin' Keith. He sure seems to know a sight o' what's goin' around."

Dornie Shaw had turned in his saddle, and his thin features had sharpened. "Shut up!" he had said coldly.

The older man had tightened and his eyes had blazed back with genuine hate, yet he had held his peace. It was educational to see how quickly he quieted down; for Poinsett, a hard, vicious man with no love for anybody or anything, obviously wanted no part of what Shaw could give him.

As the day drew on, Kedrick studied the men, and noticed they all avoided giving offense to Shaw, even the burly Fessenden who had killed twenty men and was the only one of the group Kedrick had ever seen before. He wondered if Fessenden remembered him and decided he would know before the day was out.

Around the noon camp there was less friendly banter than in a cow camp. These men were surly and touchy. Only Shaw seemed to relax much, and everything came easily for him. Clauson seemed to take over the cooking job by tacit consent, and the reason was soon obvious. He was really an excellent cook.

As he ate, Tom Kedrick studied his situation with care. He had taken this job in New Orleans, and at the time had needed money badly. Gunter had put up the cash to get him out here, and, if he did back out, he would have to find a way to repay him. Yet the more he looked over this group, the more he believed that he was into something that he wanted out of, but fast.

He had fought as a soldier of fortune in several wars. War had been his profession, and he had been a skilled fighting man almost from the beginning. His father, a one-time soldier, had a love for tactics, and Tom had grown up with an interest in things military. His education had mostly come from his father and from a newspaperman who lived with them for a winter and helped to teach the boy what he could.

Kedrick had entered the Army and fought through the Civil War. The subsequent fighting had given him a practical background to accompany his study and theory, but with all his fighting and the killing it had entailed, he had not become callous. To run a bunch of renegades off the land seemed simple enough and it promised action and excitement. It was a job he could do. Now he was no longer sure it was a job he wanted to do, for his talk with Dai Reid as well as the attitude of so many people in Mustang had convinced him that all was not as simple as it had first appeared. Now, before taking a final step, he wanted to survey the situation and see just who he would be fighting, and where. At the same time he knew the men who rode with him were going to ask few questions. They would do their killing, collect their money, and ride on.

Of them all, only Shad might think as he did, and Kedrick made a mental note to talk with the Texan before the day was over, find out where he stood and what he knew. He was inclined to agree with Shaw's original judgment, that Shad was one of the best of the lot with a gun. The man's easy way was not only natural to him, he was simply confident with that hard confidence that comes only from having measured his ability and knowing what he could do when the chips were down.

After he finished his coffee, he got to his feet and strolled over to the spring, had a drink, then arose and walked to his horse, tightening the cinch he had loosened when they stopped. The air was clear, and despite their lowered voices he could catch most of what was said.

The first question he missed, but Fessenden's reply he heard: "Don't you fret about him. He's a scrapper from way back, Dornie. I found that out. This here ain't our first meetin'."

Even at this distance and with his horse between him and the circle of men, Kedrick could sense their attention.

"Tried to finagle him out of that Patterson herd, up in Injun Territory. He didn't finagle worth a damn."

"What happened?" Goff demanded. "Any shootin'?"

"Some. I was ridin' partners with Chuck Gibbons, the Llano gunman, an' Chuck was always on the prod, sort of. One, two times I figured I might have to shoot it out with him my own self, but wasn't exactly honin' for trouble. We had too good a thing there to bust it up quarrelin'. But Chuck, he was plumb salty, an', when Kedrick faced him an' wouldn't back down or deliver the cattle, Chuck called him."

Fessenden sipped his coffee, while they waited impatiently. When they could stand the suspense no longer, Goff demanded: "Well, what happened?"

The big man shrugged. "Kedrick's here, ain't he?"

"I mean . . . what was the story?"

"Gibbons never cleared leather. None of us even seen Kedrick draw, but you could have put a half dollar over the two holes in Chuck's left shirt pocket."

Nobody spoke after that, and Tom Kedrick took his time over the cinch, then with his horse between them he walked away farther and circled, scouting the terrain thoughtfully.

He was too experienced a man to fail to appreciate how important is knowledge of terrain. All this country from Mustang to the territorial line would become a battleground in the near future, and a man's life might depend on what he knew, so he wanted an opportunity to study the country or ask questions. He had handled tough groups before, and he was not disturbed over the problem they presented, although in this case he knew the situation was much more serious. In a group they would be easier to handle than separately, for these men were individualists all, and without any group loyalty. They had faith in only two things in the last analysis: six-gun skill and money. By these they lived and by these they would die. That Fessenden had talked was pleasing, for it would settle the doubts of some of them, at least. Knowing him for a gun hand, they would more willingly accept orders from him, not because of fear, but rather because they knew him for one of their own, and not some stranger brought in for command.

When they moved out, taking their time, the heat had increased. Not a thing stirred on the wide, shallow face of the desert but a far and lonely buzzard that floated, high and alone, over a far-off mesa. Tom Kedrick's eyes roamed the country ceaselessly, and yet from time to time his thoughts kept reverting to the girl on the verandah. Connie Duane was a beautiful girl—Gunter's niece, but apparently not approving all he did. Why was she here? What was her connection with Keith? Kedrick sensed the animosity of Keith and welcomed it. A quiet man, he was slow to anger, but tough, and, when pushed, a deep-seated anger arose within him in a black tide that made him a driving fury. Knowing this rage that lay dormant within him, he rode carefully, talked carefully, and held his temper and his hand.

Dornie Shaw drew up suddenly. "This here is Largo Cañon," he said, waving his hand down the rift before them, "that peak ahead an' on your right is The Orphan. Injuns won't let no white man up there, but they say there's a spring with a good flow of water on top. Yonder begins the country in the Burwick, Keith, and Gunter buy. They don't have the land solid to the Arizona border, but they've got a big chunk of it. The center of the squatters is a town called Yellow Butte. There's maybe ten, twelve buildin's there, among 'em a store, a stable, corrals, a saloon, an' a bank."

Kedrick nodded thoughtfully. The country before him was high desert and could under no circumstances be called swamp. In the area where he stood there was little growth, a few patches of curly mesquite grass or black grama, with prickly pear, soap-weed, creosote bush, and catclaw scattered through it. In some of the washes he saw the deeper green of piñon or juniper.

They pushed on, entered the cañon, and emerged from it, heading due west. He rode warily, and once, far off on his left, he glimpsed a horseman. Later, seeing the same rider, nearer than before, he deduced they were under observation and hoped there would be no attack.

Dornie Shaw said: "The country where most of the squatters are is right smack dab in the middle o' the range the company is after. The *hombre* most likely to head 'em is Bob McLennon. He's got him two right-hand men name of Pete Slagle an' Pit Laine. Now, you asked me the other day if they would fight. Them three are shinnery oak. Slagle's an oldish feller, but McLennon's in his forties an' was once a cow-town marshal. Laine, well, he's a tough one to figure, but he packs two guns an' cuts him a wide swath over there. I hear tell he had him some gun trouble up Durango way an' he didn't need no help to handle it."

From behind him Kedrick heard a low voice mutter: " 'Most as hard to figure as his sister!"

Shaw's mouth tightened, but he gave no other evidence that he had heard, but the comment added a little to Kedrick's information. Obviously Dornie Shaw had a friend in the enemy's camp, and the information with which he had been supplying Keith must come from that source. Was the girl betraying her own brother and her friends? It could be, but could Shaw come and go among them without danger? Or did he worry himself about it? There had been no mention of Dai Reid, yet the powerful little Welshman was sure to be a figure wherever he stood, and he was definitely a man to be reckoned with.

Suddenly a rider appeared from an arroyo not thirty yards off and walked her horse toward them. Dornie Shaw swore softly and drew up. As one man, they all stopped.

The girl was small, well-made, her skin as brown as that of an Indian, her hair coal black. She had large, beautiful eyes and small hands. Her eyes flashed from Dornie to the others, then clung to Tom Kedrick, measuring him for a long minute. "Who's your friend, Dornie?" she said. "Introduce me."

Shaw's eyes were dark and hard as he turned slightly. "Cap'n Kedrick, I want you to meet Sue Laine."

"Captain?" She studied him anew. "Were you in the Army?"

"Yes," he said quietly.

Her pinto was not the horse of the rider who had been observing them; therefore, there was another rider out there somewhere. Who was he?

"You're ridin' quite a ways from home, Sue," Shaw interrupted. "You think that's wise?"

"I can take care of myself, Dornie!" Her reply was cool, and Kedrick saw blood rise under Shaw's skin. "However, I came to warn you, or Captain Kedrick, if he is in charge. It won't be safe to ride any farther. McLennon called a meeting this morning and they voted to open fire on any party of surveyors or strange riders they see. From now on, this country is closed. A rider is going to Mustang tonight with the news."

"There she is," Goff said dryly. "They are sure enough askin' for it! What if we ride on, anyway?"

She glanced at him. "Then there will be fighting," she said quietly.

"Well," Poinsett said impatiently, "what are we talkin' for? We come here to fight, didn't we? Let's ride on an' see how much battle they got in them."

Tom Kedrick studied the girl thoughtfully. She was pretty, all right, very pretty. She lacked the quiet beauty of Connie Duane, but she did have beauty. "Do they have scouts out?" he asked.

She glanced at him. "Not yet, but they will have." She smiled. "If they had, I'd never have dared ride to warn you."

"Whose side are you on, Miss Laine?" Kedrick asked.

Dornie Shaw's head came around sharply and his eyes blazed. Before he could speak, Sue Laine answered for herself: "That decision I make for myself. My brother does not make it for me, nor any one of them. They are fools! To fight over this desert!" Contemptuously she waved a hand at it. "There's no more than a bare living on it, anyway! If they lose, maybe we can leave this

102

country." She swung her horse abruptly. "Well, you've had your warning. Now I'll go back."

"I'll be ridin' your way," Shaw interposed.

Her eyes swung back to him. "Don't bother!" Then she turned her attention deliberately to Kedrick and measured him again with her cool eyes, a hint of a smile in them now. "If anybody comes, let Captain Kedrick come. They don't know him!"

Somebody in the group chuckled, and Dornie Shaw swung his horse, his face white as death. His teeth were bared, his right hand poised. "Who laughed?" he said, his voice almost trembling.

"Miss Laine," Kedrick said quietly, "I think Dornie Shaw could make the trip better than I. He knows the country."

Shaw's eyes glittered. "I asked . . . *who laughed?*"

Kedrick turned his head. "Forget it, Shaw." His voice was crisp. "There'll be no fighting with other men in the outfit while I'm in command!"

For an instant, Dornie Shaw held his pose, then his eyes, suddenly opaque as a rattler's, swung toward Kedrick. "You're tellin' *me?*" Incredulity was mixed with sarcasm.

Tom Kedrick knew danger when he saw it, but he only nodded. "You, or anybody, Dornie. We have a job to do. You've hired me for that job as much as any man here. If we begin to fight among ourselves, we'll get nothing done, and right now we can't afford to lose a good man. I scarcely think," he added, "that either Keith or Burwick would like the idea of a killing among their own men."

Shaw's eyes held Kedrick's and for an instant there was no sound. A cicada hummed in the brush, and Sue Laine's horse stamped at a fly. Tom Kedrick knew in that instant that Dornie Shaw hated him, and he had an idea that this was the first time Shaw had ever been thwarted in any purpose he held.

Then Shaw's right hand slowly lowered. "You got me on that one, Cap'n." His voice was empty, dry. "I reckon this is too soon to start shootin' . . . an' old man Burwick is right touchy."

Sue Laine glanced again at Kedrick, genuine surprise and not a little respect in her eyes. "I'll be going. Watch yourselves!"

Before her horse could more than start, Kedrick asked: "Miss Laine, which of your outfit rides a long-legged grulla?"

She turned on him, her face pale as death. "A . . . a grulla?"

"Yes," he said, "such a rider has been watching us most of the morning, and such a rider is not over a half mile away now. Also," he added, "he has a field glass!"

Fessenden turned with an oath, and Poinsett glared around. Only Shaw spoke. His voice was strained and queer. "A grulla? Here?"

104

He refused to say more, but Kedrick studied him, puzzled by the remark. It was almost as if Shaw knew the grulla horse, but had not expected it to be seen here. The same might be true of Sue Laine, obviously upset by his comment. Long after they rode on, turning back toward the spring on the North Fork, Kedrick puzzled over it. This was an entirely new element that might mean anything or nothing.

There was little talking on the way back. Poinsett was obviously irritated that they had not ridden on in, yet he seemed content enough to settle down into another camp.

IV

Dornie Shaw was silent, saying nothing at all. Only when Tom Kedrick arose after supper and began to saddle his horse did he look up. Kedrick glanced at him. "Shaw, I'm ridin' to Yellow Butte. I'm going to look that set-up over first-hand. I don't want trouble, an' I'm not huntin' any, but I want to know what we're tacklin'."

Shaw was standing, staring after him, when he rode off. He rode swiftly, pushing due west at a good pace to take advantage of the remaining light. He had more than one reason for the ride. He wanted to study the town and the terrain, but also he wanted to see what the people were like.

Were they family men? Or were they outlaws? He had seen little thus far that tended to prove the outlaw theory.

The town of Yellow Butte lay huddled at the base of the long, oval-shaped mesa from which it took its name. There, on a bit of flat land, the stone and frame buildings of the town had gathered together. Most of them backed against the higher land behind them, and faced toward the arroyo. Only three buildings and the corrals were on the arroyo side, but one thing was obvious. The town had never been planned for defense.

A rifleman or two on top of Yellow Butte could cover any movement in the village, and the town was exposed to fire from both the high ground behind the town and the bed of the arroyo where there was shelter under its banks. The butte itself was scarcely one hundred and fifty feet higher than the town and looked right down the wide street before the buildings.

Obviously, however, some move had been made toward defense, or was in the process of being made, for there were some piles of earth, plainly from recent digging, near several of the buildings. He studied them, puzzled over their origin and cause. Finally he gave up and scouted the area.

He glanced at the butte thoughtfully. Had they thought of putting their own riflemen up there? It would seem the obvious thing, yet more than one competent commander had forgotten the obvious at some time during his career, and it might also be true of these men. The top of the butte not only commanded the town, but most of the country around, and was the highest point within several miles.

That could come later. Now Kedrick turned his Appaloosa down the hill toward the town, riding in the open, his right hand hanging free at his side. Yet, if he was seen, nothing was done to disturb him. How would it have been if there were more than one rider?

He swung down before the Butte Saloon, and tied his horse at the rail. The animal was weary, he knew, and in no shape for a long ride, but he had made his own plans and they did not require such a ride. The street was empty, so he stepped up on the walk and pushed through the swinging doors into the bright lights of the interior. A man sitting alone at a table saw him, scowled, and started to speak, then went on with his solitaire. Tom Kedrick crossed to the bar. "Rye," he said quietly.

The bartender nodded and, without looking up, poured the drink. It was not until Kedrick dropped his coin on the bar that he did raise his glance. Instantly his face stiffened: "Who're you?" he demanded. "I never saw you before!"

Kedrick was aware that men had closed in on

both sides of him, both of them strangers. One was a sharp-looking, oldish man, the other an obviously belligerent redhead. "Pour a drink for my friends, too," he said, and then he turned slowly, so they would not mistake his intentions, until his back was to the bar. Carefully he surveyed the room. There were a dozen men here, and all eyes were on him. "I'm buying," he said quietly. "Will you gentlemen join me?"

Nobody moved, and he shrugged. He turned back to the bar. His drink was gone.

Slowly he lifted his eyes to the bartender. "I bought a drink," he said quietly.

The man stared back at him, his eyes hard. "Never noticed it," he said.

"I bought a drink, paid my money, and I want my drink."

All was still. The men on either side of him leaned on the bar, ignoring him.

"I'm a patient man," he persisted, "I bought a drink, an' I want it . . . now."

"Mister"—the bartender thrust his wide face across the bar—"we don't serve drinks to your kind here. Now get out before we throw you out!"

Kedrick's forearms were resting on the edge of the bar, and what happened was done so swiftly that neither man beside him had a chance to move. Tom Kedrick's right hand shot out and grabbed the bartender by the shirt collar under his chin, then he turned swiftly back to the bar, and heaved! The bartender came over the bar as if greased and hit the floor with a crash. Instantly Kedrick spun away from the two men beside him and stood facing the room, gun in hand.

Men had started to their feet, and several had moved toward him. Now they froze where they were. The .44 Russian had appeared as if materialized from thin air.

"Gentlemen," Kedrick said quietly, "I did not come here hunting trouble. I have been hired for a job as all of you, at some time or another, have been hired for a job. I came to see if you were the manner of men you have been represented as being. Evidently your bartender is hard of hearing, or lacking in true hospitality. I ordered a drink. You"—Kedrick gestured at the man playing solitaire—"look like a man of judgment. You pour my drink and pour it on the end of the bar nearest me. Then"—his eyes held the room—"pour each of these gentlemen a drink." With his left hand he extracted a gold eagle from his pocket and slapped it on the bar. "That pays."

He took another step back, then coolly he holstered his gun. Eyes studied him, but nobody moved. The redhead did not like it. He had an urge to show how tough he was and Kedrick could see it building. "You!" Kedrick asked quickly. "Are you married? Children?"

The redhead stared at him, then said, his voice surly: "Yeah, I'm married, and I got two kids. What's it to you?"

"I told you," Kedrick replied evenly. "I came to see what manner of men you are."

The man who was pouring the drinks looked up. "I'll answer your questions. I'm Pete Slagle."

"I've heard of you."

A slight smile came to Slagle's mouth. "Yeah," he said, "an' I've heard of you."

Nobody moved or spoke while Slagle calmly poured the drinks, then he straightened and glanced around the room. "Men," he said, "I reckon there's no use goin' off half-cocked an' gettin' somebody killed. Let's give this man a chance to speak his piece. We sure don't have to buy what he wants to sell us if we don't like his argument."

"Thanks, Slagle." Kedrick studied the room. Two of the faces seemed hard, unrelenting. Another was genuinely interested, but at the door in the rear a man loitered who had shifty eyes and a sour face. He could have been, in disposition at least, a twin brother to the former outlaw, Clauson.

"The land around here," Kedrick said quietly, "is about to be purchased from the government by the firm who has employed me. The firm of Burwick, Keith, and Gunter. In New Orleans, where I was hired, I was told that there were squatters on the land, a bunch of outlaws, renegades, and wasters, that they would resist being put off, and would aim to keep the badlands for themselves. My job was to clean them out, to clear the land for the company. I have come here for that purpose."

There was a low murmur from the back of the room. Kedrick took time to toss off his drink and then calmly begin to roll a smoke. To his right, the door opened and two men came in. One of these was as tall as himself with coal-black hair turning gray at the temples. His eyes were gray and cold, his face firmly cut. He glanced sharply around the room, then at Kedrick.

"Cap'n Tom Kedrick, Bob," Slagle said quietly, "speakin' his piece. He's just explained that we've been represented as a bunch of renegades."

"That sounds like Burwick," McLennon said. "Get on with it, Kedrick."

"I've little to say but this. Naturally, like any good fighting man, I wanted to look over the terrain. Moreover, since arriving in Mustang, certain rumors and hints have reached me that the picture is not one-sided. I have come out here to look you over, to see exactly what sort of people you are, and if you are the outlaws and wasters you have been represented to be. Also, I would like to have a statement from you."

Red's face was ugly. "We got nothin' to say to you, Kedrick," he said harshly, "nothin' at all!

Just you come down here with your killers an' see how many get away alive!"

"Wait a minute, Red!" Slagle interrupted. "Let Tom have his say."

"Aw, why bother?" Red said roughly. "The man is scared or he'd never have come huntin' information!"

Kedrick's eyes held Red's thoughtfully, and he said slowly: "No, Red, I'm not scared. If I decide the company is right and you are to be run off, that is exactly what I'll do. If the men I have are not enough, I'll get more. I'm used to war, Red. I've been at it all my life, and I know how to win. I'm not here because I'm scared. I have come simply because I make a pass at being a just man. If you have a just claim to your places here, and are not as represented, I'll step out of this.

"Naturally," he added, "I can't speak for the others, but I will advise them as to my conclusions."

"Fair enough," McLennon agreed. "All right, I'll state our case. This land is government land like all of it. The Navajos an' Utes claim some of it, an' some of us have dickered with them for land. We've moved in an' settled on this land. Four or five of us have been here upward of ten years, most of us have been here more than three. We've barns built, springs cleaned out, some fences. We've stocked some land, lived through a few bad summers and worse winters.

112

Some of us have wives, an' some of us children. We're makin' homes here. The company is tryin' to gyp us. The law says we were to have six months' notice. That is, it was to be posted six months before the sale by the government to the company. This land, as we understand it, is supposed to be unoccupied. Well, it isn't. We live on it. Moreover, that notice was posted five months ago, stuck in out-of-the-way places, in print so fine a man can scarcely read it without a magnifyin' glass. A month ago one of the boys read it, but it took him a few days to sort out the meanin' of the legal phrasin', and then he hightailed it to me. We ain't got the money to send a man to the government. So all we can do is fight. That's what we figure on. If the company runs us off, which I don't figure you or nobody can do, they'll buy ever' inch of it with their blood, believe me."

A murmur of appreciation went through the room, and Kedrick scanned their faces thoughtfully. Dornie Shaw had judged these men correctly. They would fight. Moreover, with men like McLennon and Slagle to lead them, they would be hard to handle. Legally the company seemed to be in the best position; the squatters were bucking a stacked deck. From here it would take a man all of two weeks, and possibly three, even to get to Washington, let alone cut through all the government red tape to get to the men who could block the sale—if it could be blocked.

"This here's a speculation on their part," McLennon stated. "There's rumor this here land is goin' into an Injun reservation, an', if it does, that means they'll stick the government a nice price for the land."

"Or you will," Kedrick replied. "Looks like there's two sides to this question, McLennon. The company has an argument. If the federal government does make this a reservation, you'll have to move, anyway."

"We'll face that when it comes," Slagle said. "Right now we're buckin' the company. Our folks aren't speculators. We aren't gunmen, either."

Another man had entered the room, and Kedrick spotted him instantly. It was Burt, the big man he had whipped in the street fight. The man stopped by the wall, and surveyed the room.

"None of you?" Kedrick asked gently. "I have heard some stories about Pit Laine."

"Laine's a good man!" Red burst out heatedly. "He'll do to ride any river with!"

Neither McLennon nor Slagle spoke, and the latter shifted his feet uneasily. Evidently there was a difference of opinion here. He made a note to check on Laine, to find out more about him.

"Well," Kedrick said finally, "I reckon I'll study it a little. In the meantime, let's keep the peace. I'll keep my men off, if you will do likewise."

"We aren't huntin' trouble," McLennon said.

"As long as there's no shootin' at us, an' as long as the company men stay off our land, there'll be no trouble from us."

"Fact is," Slagle said, "we sent Roberts ridin' in with a message to Burwick to that effect. We ain't huntin' for no trouble."

Kedrick turned toward the door, but the bartender's voice stopped him. "You forgot your change," he said dryly.

Kedrick glanced at him, grinned, then picked it up. "Be seein' you," he said, and stepped to the door.

At that instant, the door burst open and a man staggered into the room, his arm about another man, who he dropped to the floor. "Roberts!" the man said. "He's been murdered!"

All eyes stared at the man on the floor. That he had been shot many times was obvious. He had also been ridden over, for his body was torn and beaten by the hoofs of running horses. Tom Kedrick felt his stomach turn over. Sick with pity and shock, he lifted his eyes. He looked up into a circle of accusation: McLennon, shocked and unbelieving, Slagle, horrified. Red pointed a finger that trembled with anger. "While he stands an' talks to us, his outfit murders Bob!"

"Git him!" somebody yelled. "Git him! I got a rope!"

Kedrick was standing at the door, and he knew there was no reasoning with these men. Later, they might think and reason that he might have known nothing about the killing of Roberts. Now, they would not listen. As the man yelled, he hurled himself through the swinging doors and, jerking loose his reins, hit the saddle of the Appaloosa. The startled horse swung and lined out, not down the street, but between the buildings.

Behind him men shouted and cursed. A shot rang out, and he heard a bullet clip past his head as he swung between buildings. Then he knew his escape had driven him into a *cul-de-sac*, for he was now facing, not more than two hundred yards away, the rim around the flat where the town lay. Whether there was a break in that wall he could not guess, but he had an idea both the route upstream and that downstream of the arroyo would be covered by guards, so he swung his horse and charged into the darkness toward Yellow Butte itself.

As he had come into town, he had seemed to see a V-shaped opening near its base. Whether there was a cut through the rim there he did not know. It might only be a box cañon, and a worse trap than the one into which he had run on his first break.

He slowed his pace, knowing that silence was the first necessity now, for, if they heard him, he could easily be bottled up. The flat was small, and aside from crossing the arroyo there were but two routes of escape, and both would be watched, as he had first surmised. The butte towered high above him now, and his horse walked softly in the abysmal darkness of its foot. His safety was a matter of minutes, for they must know they had him.

The Appaloosa was tired, he knew, for he had been going all day, and the day had been warm and he was a big man. He was in no shape for a hard run against fresh horses, so the only possible escape lay in some shrewd move that would have them guessing and give him time. Yet he must be gone before daylight or he was through. By day they would comb this area and surely discover him.

Now the cañon mouth yawned before him. The walls were not high but were deep enough to allow no escape on horseback, at least. The shouts of pursuit had stopped, but he knew they were hard at work to find him. By now they would know from the guards on the stream that he was still on the flat, and had not escaped. Those guards might be creatures of his own imagination, but knowing the men with whom he dealt, he was shrewd enough to realize that, if they had not guarded the openings before his arrival, they certainly would have sent guards out at once.

The cañon was narrow and he rode on, moving with extreme caution, yet when he had gone but a short distance, he saw the end of the cañon rising above him, black and somber. His throat tightened and his mouth went dry. The Appaloosa stopped and Tom Kedrick sat silently, feeling the labored breathing of the horse and knowing this was an end. He was trapped. Fairly trapped!

Behind him, a light flared briefly, then went out, but there was a shout. That had been a struck match, somebody looking for tracks. And they had found them. In a few minutes more, for they would move cautiously, they would be here. There would be no reasoning with them now. They had him. He was trapped.

V

Captain Tom Kedrick sat very still, listening. He heard some gravel stir; a stone rattled down the cañon. Every move would count now, and he must take no unnecessary chance. He was cornered, and while he did not want to kill any of these men, he had no intention of being killed.

Carefully he dismounted. As his boot touched the sand, he tested it to make sure no sound would result when his weight settled. Haste now was his greatest danger. There might be nothing he could do, but he was a man of many experiences, and in the past there had always been a way out.

Usually there was if a man took his time and kept his head.

Standing still beside the Appaloosa, he studied the situation. His eyes had grown accustomed to the darkness under the bulk of Yellow Butte. He stared around, seeing the faint gray of sand underfoot, the black bulk of boulders, and the more ragged bulk of underbrush. Leading his horse, he followed a narrow strip of gray that showed an opening between boulders. Scarcely wide enough to admit his horse, the opening led back for some twenty feet, then widened. These were low boulders, rising scarcely above his waist, with the brush somewhat higher. The horse seemed to sense the danger, for it, too, walked quietly and almost without sound.

Literally he was feeling his way in the dark, but that trail of sand must come from somewhere, for water had run here, and that water might spill off the cliff edge, or might come through some opening. Walking steadily, he found himself going deeper into a tangle of boulders, weaving his way along that thin gray trail, into he knew not what.

Twice he paused and, with his hat, worked back along the path brushing out the tracks. He could not see how good a job he was doing, but the opening was narrow enough to give him a good chance of success. When he had pushed back into the tangle for all of ten minutes, he was brought up sharply by the cliff itself. He had found his way up the slope, through the talus, brush, and scattered boulders, to the very face of the rock. Above him, and apparently out of reach, was a notch in the cliff, and this was probably the source of the sandy trail he had followed. Worried now, he ground-hitched the Appaloosa and moved along the cliff, feeling his way along the face, searching each crack.

To his left, he found nothing. Several times he paused to listen, but no sound came from down the cañon. If this were a box cañon, with no exit, they would probably know it and make no attempt to close in until daylight. In the darkness a man could put up quite a fight in here. Yet, because of their eagerness to avenge the dead man, they might push on. Speaking softly to the horse, he worked his way along the face to the right, but here the pile of talus fell off sharply and he dipped into a hollow. It was cool and the air felt damp. There might even be a spring there, but he heard no water running.

Despite the coolness he was sweating, and he paused, mopping his face and listening. As he stood there, he felt a faint breath of wind against his cheek! He stiffened with surprise, then with a sudden surge of hope he turned and eagerly explored the rocky face, but could find no source for that breeze. He started on, moving more cautiously, then the talus began to steepen under his feet, so he worked his way up the cliff alone. He carried with him his rifle.

At the top he could turn and glance back down the cañon and the faint grayness in the distance that indicated the way he had come. Here the cañon turned a bit, ending in a sort of blind alley on an angle from the true direction of the cañon. There, breaking the edge of the cliff above him, was a notch, and a steep slide led to the top! It must have been some vague stirring of wind from up there on the rim that had touched his cheek, but the slide was steeper than a stairway, and might start sliding underfoot. Certainly the rattle would give away his attempt, and it would be the matter of a few minutes only for them to circle around. As far as that went, they could even now be patrolling the rim above him.

Turning, his foot went from under him and only a frenzied grasp at some brush kept him from falling into whatever hole he had stumbled upon. Scrambling back to good footing, he dropped a pebble and heard it strike some fifteen or twenty feet down. Working his way along the edge, he reached the foot of the slide, or nearly there, and knew what he had come upon. Water, flooding down that slide during heavy rains, had struck a soft stratum of sand or mud at this point and, striking it with force, had gouged out a deep hole that probably ran back into the cañon itself. There was always a chance that deep within this crack there might be some hiding place, some concealment. Turning abruptly, he returned for his horse.

The slide continued steeply to the bottom of the crevasse scooped from the earth, and, when they reached bottom, he glanced up. He was walking, leading the horse, but the opening of the hole in which he stood was at least fifteen feet above him, and not more than seven or eight feet in width. He moved on into it, and after only a short distance it was almost covered on top by a thick growth of brush growing on the surface or from the sides near the top.

It was cool and still down here, and he pushed on until he found a spot where the rush of water had made a turn, and had gouged deeply under the bank, making a sort of cave beneath the overhang. Into this he led his horse, and here he stopped. A little water stood at the deepest part of the turn, and he allowed the Appaloosa to drink. When the horse had finished, the shallow pool was gone.

Kedrick tried the water in his canteen, then stripped the saddle from the horse, and rubbed him down with a handful of coarse grass. Then he tied the horse and, spreading his blanket, rolled up in it. He was philosophical. He had done what he could. If they found him now, there was nothing to do but shoot it out where he was.

Surprisingly he slept, and when he awakened,

it was the startled breathing of the Appaloosa that warned him. Instantly he was on his feet, speaking in a whisper to the horse and resting his hand on its shoulder. Day had come, and somewhere above them, yet some distance, there were voices!

The cave in which he stood was sandstone, no more than fifteen feet in depth, and probably eight feet high at the opening. Kedrick moved to the mouth, studied the crevasse down which he had come, and it was as he had supposed, a deep-cut watercourse from the notch in the cliff. Evidently during heavy rains this roared full of water, almost to the brim.

At the place where he now stood, the brush on either side almost met over the top, and at one point a fallen slab bridged the crack. Glancing back the way he had come, Kedrick saw that much of it was also covered by brush, and there was a chance that he would not be found. A very, very slim chance, but a chance. He could ask for no more.

He wanted to smoke, but dared not, for the smell of it might warn them of his presence. Several times he heard voices, some of them quite near. He glanced toward the back of the cave and saw the gelding drinking again. Evidently the water had seeped through during the night, even though not much. His canteen was over half full, and as yet water was not a problem.

His rifle across his knees, he waited, from time to time staring down the crevasse in the direction he had been going. Where did this water flow? It must flow into the arroyo below, near town, and in that case they would certainly know of it. The men and women of the town might not know of it, but the children would without doubt. Trust them to find every cave, every niche in the rock within miles.

Yet as the morning wore on, although he heard occasionally the sound of voices, nobody approached his place of concealment, nor did they seem aware of it. Once, he ventured out into the crevasse itself, and pulled a few handfuls of grass growing on a slight mound of earth. This he fed to the horse, that ate gratefully. He dug some jerky from his own pack and chewed on it, wishing for a cup of coffee.

Later, he ventured farther down the crevasse which seemed to dip steeply from where he was, and, hearing no voices, he pushed on, coming to a point where the crevasse turned sharply again, the force of the water having hollowed out a huge cave like a bowl standing on edge, and then the water turned and shot down an even steeper declivity into the black maw of a cavern.

Having come this far, he took a chance on leaving his horse alone and walked on down toward the cave. The entrance was high and wide and the cave extended deep into the mountain with several shelves or ledges that seemed to show no signs of water. There was a pool in the bottom, and apparently the water filled a large basin, but lost itself through some cracks in the bottom of the larger hollow. Although he penetrated no great distance, he could find no evidence of another outlet, nor could he feel any motion of air. Yet, as he looked around him, he realized that with some food a man might well hide in this place for weeks, and, unless they went to the foot of the slide and found the opening into the crevasse, this place might never be discovered. The run-off from the cliff, then, did not go to the arroyo, but ended here, in this deep cavern.

The day wore on slowly, and twice he walked back down to the cavern to smoke, but left his horse where it was, for he had an idea he could escape later. Yet when dusk came, and he worked his way back up the crevasse slide, he crawled out on the edge where he could look toward the entrance and saw two men, squatting there beside a fire, with rifles under their hands. They believed him concealed inside, and hoped to starve him out.

By this time Dornie Shaw must have returned to Mustang with news of his disappearance and, probably, of their murder of the messenger. For he was sure that it had been his own group who had committed the crime. It was scarcely likely that Gunter or Keith would countenance such a thing near town where it would not fail to be seen and reported upon by unfriendly witnesses.

Returning, he studied the slide to the rim. It was barely possible that a horse might scramble up there. It would be no trick for an active man, and the Appaloosa was probably a mountain horse. It was worth a gamble—if there was no one on top to greet him. Pulling an armful of grass from near the brush and boulders, he returned to the horse, and watched it gratefully munch the rich green grass.

Connie Duane was disturbed. She had seen the messenger come to her uncle and the others, and had heard their reply. Then, at almost noon the following day, Dornie Shaw and the others had come in, and they had returned without Tom Kedrick. Why that should disturb her she could not have said, but the fact remained that it did. Since he had stepped up on the verandah, she had thought of little else, remembering the set of his chin, the way he carried his shoulders, and the startled expression when he saw her. There was something about him that was different, not only from the men around her uncle, but from any man she had known before. Now, when despite herself she had looked forward to his return, he was missing.

John Gunter came out on the verandah,

nervously biting the end from a cigar. "What happened?" she asked. "Is something wrong? Where's Captain Kedrick?"

"Wish I knew!" His voice was sharp with anxiety. "He took a ride to look over those squatters an' never came back. I don't trust Shaw, no matter how much Keith does. He's too bloodthirsty. We could get into a lot of trouble here, Connie. That's why I wanted Kedrick. He has judgment, brains."

"Perhaps he decided he wanted no part of it, Uncle. Maybe he decided your squatters were not outlaws or renegades."

Gunter glanced at her sharply. "Who has been talking to you?" he demanded.

"No one. It hasn't been necessary. I have walked around town, and I've seen some of these outlaws, as you call them, have wives and children, that they buy supplies, and look like nice people. I don't like it, Uncle John, and I don't like to think that my money may be financing a part of it."

"Now, now! Don't bother your head over it. You may be sure that Loren and I will do everything we can for your best interests."

"Then drop the whole thing!" she pleaded. "There's no need for it. I've money enough, and I don't want money that comes from depriving others of their homes. They all have a right to live, a chance."

"Of course!" Gunter was impatient. "We've gone over all this before! But I tell you most of these people are trash, and no matter about that, they all will be put off that land, anyway. The government is going to buy out whoever has control. That will mean us, and that means we'll get a nice, juicy profit."

"From the government? Your own government, Uncle?" Connie studied him coolly. "I fail to understand the sort of man who will attempt to defraud his own government. There are people like that, I suppose, but somehow I never thought I'd find one in my own family."

"Don't be silly, child. You know nothing of business . . . you aren't practical."

"I suppose not. Only I seem to remember that a lot of worthwhile things don't seem practical at the moment. No, I believe I'll withdraw my investment in this deal and buy a small ranch somewhere nearby. I will have no part in it."

"You can't do that!" Gunter exploded impatiently. "Your money is already in, and there's no way of getting it out until this business is closed. Now, why don't you trust me like a good girl? You always have before!"

"Yes, I have, Uncle John, but I never believed you could be dishonest." She studied him frankly. "You aren't very happy about this yourself. You know," she persisted, "those people aren't going to move without a fight. You believed they could be frightened. Well, they can't. I've seen Bob McLennon, and he's not the kind of man who can be frightened. Even by that choice bunch of murderers Loren has gathered together."

"They aren't that. Not murderers," Gunter protested uneasily, but refused to meet her eyes. "Reckless, yes. And temperamental. Not murderers."

"Not even Dornie Shaw? The nice-looking, boyish one who has killed a dozen men and is so cold-blooded and fiendish at times that others are afraid of him? No, Uncle, there is no way you can side-step this. If you continue, you are going to countenance murder and the killing of innocent people. Loren doesn't care. He has always been cold-blooded. You've wondered why I wouldn't marry him. That's why. He has the disposition of a tiger. He would kill anything or anyone that stood in his way. Even you, Uncle John."

He started and looked at her uneasily. "Why did you say that?"

"Because it's true. I know our tall and handsome man. He will allow nothing to come between him and what he desires. You've chosen some choice companions." She got to her feet. "If you hear anything of Captain Kedrick, let me know, will you?"

Gunter stood still for a long time after she left. He swore bitterly. Connie was like her mother. She always had the faculty for putting her finger on the truth, and certainly she was right about this. It was beginning to look ugly, but way down deep in his heart he was upset less over Keith than over Burwick. That strange, fat, and dirty man was a thing of evil, of corruption. There was some evil thing within him, something cold and vicious as a striking snake. Connie Duane was not the only person who was disturbed over the strange disappearance of Tom Kedrick.

Bob McLennon, unofficial commander of the forces for defense, sat in his rambling ranch house on the edge of Yellow Butte. Pete Slagle, Burt Williams, Dai Reid, and Pit Laine were all gathered there. With them was Sue Laine, keeping in the background. Her dark, lively eyes were stirring from one to the other, her ears were alert for every word.

"Blazes, man!" McLennon said irritably. "Where could he have gone? I'd have sworn he went into that box cañon. There was no other place for him to go, unless he took wings and flew. He had to go in there!"

"You looked yourself," Slagle said dryly. "Did you see him? He just ain't there, that's all. He got plumb away!"

"He probably did that," Dai Reid commented. "A quick man, that Tom Kedrick. Hand or mind, he's quick." He drew out his pipe and stoked it slowly. "You shouldn't have jumped him," he continued. "I know the lad, an' he's honest. If he said that was what he come for, it was the truth he told. I'd take any oath he'd no knowledge of the killin'!"

"I'd like to believe that," McLennon agreed. "The man impressed me. We could use an honest man on the other side, one who would temper the wind a bit, or get this thing stopped."

"It won't be that Shaw who stops. He's a murderin' little devil," Slagle said. "He'll kill like a weasel in a chicken pen until there's naught left to kill."

"Kedrick fought me fair," Williams said. "I'll give him that."

"He's a fair man," Dai persisted. "Since a lad I've known him. I'd not be wrong. I'd give fifty acres of my holdin' for the chance to talk to him."

Daylight brought the first attack. It came swiftly, a tight bunch of riders that exploded from the mouth of the arroyo hit the dusty street of Yellow Butte on a dead run, pistols firing, and then the deep, heavy concussion of dynamite. As suddenly as they had come, they were gone. Two men sprawled in the street.

Peters, the man Shaw had faced down in the street of Mustang, was one of them. He had taken three .44 slugs through the chest and died before he hit the ground. He had made one final effort to win back his self-respect. He had seen Dornie

Shaw in the van of the charging riders and rushed into the street to get him. He failed to get off a single shot. The second man down was shot through the thigh and arm. He was a Swede who had just put in his second crop.

The riders had planned their attack well and had worked near enough to the guards at the mouth of the arroyo, and at a time when no attack was expected. The one guard awake was knocked down by a charging horse, but miraculously suffered only bruises. Two bundles of dynamite had been thrown. One had exploded against the door of the general store, smashing it off its hinges and tearing up the porch. The sound exploded harmlessly between the buildings.

The first rattle of rifle fire brought Tom Kedrick to an observation point. He had saddled his horse, hoping for a break, and instantly he saw it. The two guards had rushed in to the scene of action, and he led his horse out of the crevasse, rode at a canter to the cañon's mouth, and, seeing dust over the town, he swung right and, skirting close to the butte, slipped out into the open, a free man once more.

VI

Kedrick did not return to Mustang. He had come this far for a purpose, and he meant to achieve it. Turning west and north, he rode upstream away from Yellow Butte and Mustang. He wanted actually to see some of the homes of which so much had been said. By the way these people lived he could tell the sort they were. It was still and warm in the morning, and after the preliminary escape he slowed his horse to a walk and studied the terrain.

Certainly nothing could be further from swampland, and in that at least the company had misrepresented. Obviously they had misrepresented in maintaining that the land was vacant, but, if the squatters were a shiftless lot, Kedrick knew he would continue his job. Already he was heartily sick of the whole mess, yet he owed Gunter money, and how to pay it back was a bigger problem. And then, although the idea lurked almost unthought in the back of his consciousness, there was Connie Duane.

In his fast-moving and active life he had met many women, and a few had interested him, but none so much as this tall girl with the quiet, interested eyes. His desire to get back to Mustang had nothing to do with the company, but only with her. At the same time, Dornie Shaw had acted without his orders, had slain the messenger, and attacked the town. Of course, they might think him dead.

Turning due north, he rode though the sage-brush and catclaw toward two towering blue mountains that stood along this side of the rim that bordered the country to the north. On his left, he saw broken land, and what was evidently a deep arroyo. He swung the Appaloosa over and headed it toward the cañon. Suddenly he reined in.

On the ground before him were the tracks of a trotting horse, and he recognized them. They were the same tracks left by the strange rider on the grulla mustang that had scouted their approach to Yellow Butte. The tracks were fresh.

Riding more slowly, he came to the edge of the cañon and looked down at a long, green meadow, fenced and watered by a small stream. At the far side, tucked in a corner, was a stone cottage, at once more attractive and better built than any other he had seen in this section. Ahead of him a trail turned down, so without delay he rode down it and walked his horse across the meadow by a narrow lane, toward the house.

It was a pleasant place of sandstone blocks and a thatched roof. Shade trees sheltered the yard, and there were a half dozen hens pecking about. In the corral there were several horses. His heart jumped as he saw the grulla, saddled and waiting.

He drew up in the courtyard and swung down, trailing his reins. The door opened and a girl came out with a pan of water. She started as she saw him, and he recognized her instantly. It was Sue Laine, the girl of the trail, the girl in whom Dornie was reported to be interested.

"You!" she gasped as she stared at him. "They told me you were dead!"

He shrugged. "Not dead, just hungry. Could you feed a man?"

She studied him a minute, then nodded. "Come in. Better tie your horse, though. He'll head for that meadow if you don't. And"—her voice was dry—"you may need him. This isn't exactly friendly country."

He tied his horse near the grulla and followed her inside. "Isn't it?" he said. "Somehow I gathered you weren't exactly an enemy to the company."

"Don't say that!" she flared. "Don't ever say that!" Her voice lowered. "Not around here, anyway. If my brother ever heard . . ."

So Pit Laine and his sister did not see alike? That was an interesting point. He bathed his hands and face in the basin she left him, then combed his hair. Ruefully he rubbed his chin. "Your brother got a razor? I hate to go unshaven."

She brought a razor without comment, and he shaved, then dried his face and hands, and walked

135

into the house. It was amazingly neat, and on a side table there were several books. Flowered curtains hung at the windows, and several copper dishes were burnished to brightness. He sat down and she brought him food—beef, eggs, and homemade bread with honey.

"Everybody's looking for you," she said. "Where have you been?"

He accepted the statement and ignored the question. "After that messenger was killed, I had to get out of Yellow Butte. I did. What's been happening?"

"Keith served a final ultimatum. We either move, or they run us out. McLennon refused."

"He did right."

She turned on him, her eyes questioning. "You think that? I thought you were their man?"

He looked up from his food, and shook his head. "I don't know where I stand, but I don't go for murder, nor for running people out of their homes."

"They can't stay, anyway. If this land becomes a reservation, they will all be moved off. We will, too. They are foolish to fight."

"At least the government will buy their land and pay for their investment. In any event, the company has misrepresented things."

"Does it matter?" She sat down opposite him. "They will win. They have money, influence, and power. The settlers here have nothing." She looked around bitterly. "Perhaps you think I am going against my own people, but that's not true. These aren't my people. Pit and I don't belong here and we never have, although Pit won't see it. Do you think I want to slave my life away on this desert?" She leaned toward him. "Look, Captain Kedrick, you're one of them, not just working for them, not just a hired gunman like Dornie Shaw. You can lead the men you have to, and I wouldn't be surprised but that you could even handle Keith. You could be a big man in this country, or any country. Why be foolish and start thinking like you are? These farmers and ranchers can do nothing for you. They can't even help themselves. The company will win, and, if you are one of them, you will have a share in the winning. Don't get foolish, Captain, stay with them, do what you have to do."

"There are things more important than money. There's self-respect."

She stared at him, her eyes widening. "You don't really believe that? Try buying supplies with it, sometime. You won't get any place. But that isn't the point. You'll do what you want, but I want a man who will take me out of this desert." She got up quickly and came around the table. "You could do it, Captain. You could become rich, right here."

He smiled at her. "Ambitious, aren't you?"

"Why not? Being a rancher's wife doesn't

appeal to me. I want to get away from here, go some place, be something, and enjoy life." She hesitated, studying him. "You could edge Gunter out of it, and Keith . . . maybe even Burwick. But the first two would be easy, and I know how."

"You do?" He looked up at her. She stood very close to him, and she was smiling down at him. She was, he had to admit, a lovely girl, and an exciting one. Too exciting for comfort right now, and that was a fact she understood completely. "How?"

She shook her head. "Oh, no! That I'd tell you only if you threw in with me, joined me. But this much I'll tell you . . . John Gunter is small potatoes. They needed money, and he had that girl's money, so they roped him in. Keith is dangerous because he is ambitious and unscrupulous, but the man to reckon with is Burwick. He will be top man when this thing is over, and you can bank on it, he has a way figured, all the time!"

"You seem to know a great deal."

"I do. Men like me, and men talk. They don't have any idea how much I lead them to say, or how much I remember."

"Why tell me all this?"

"Because you're the man who can do what has to be done. You could whip that bunch into line. All of them would listen to you, even Dornie Shaw . . . and he's suspicious of you."

"Of me? Why?"

"He saw Dai Reid come from your room. He was watching you."

So that was it! He had suspected that Shaw had something on his mind. But why had Shaw been watching? What was the little gunman thinking of? And had he reported that conference to Keith?

Kedrick finished his meal and lighted a cigarette. Ever since their first meeting in the desert, this girl had puzzled him. He was inclined to doubt if any girl, reared as she must have been, could be so sincerely disdaining of all loyalty and so plainly self-seeking. And this girl was scarcely more than a child, slim, brown, and lovely, with her quick, measuring eyes and her soft lips. Now, she seemed to have selected him for the man who was to take her away from the desert. But how many others had the same idea? And then, he had no idea of leaving the desert.

"Your brother around?" he asked.

Her glance was a quick flash of alarm. "You don't want to see him, or talk to him. You'd better get out of here."

"On the contrary, Sue, I'd like to talk to Pit. I've heard about him and I'd like to know him."

"You'd better go," she warned. "He'll be back soon, and some of that Yellow Butte crowd may be with him."

"You mean he's not here? Then whose horse is that out there? That grulla?"

Her face was strange as she shook her head. "You'll think I'm a liar, but I don't know. I never saw the rider."

His eyes searched hers. He could see nothing but sincerity there, sincerity and a little fear. "You mean that horse showed up there, tied like that? And you never saw the rider?"

"That's right. I looked out this morning, shortly after Pit left, and he was tied right there. This isn't the first time. He has been here twice before, when Pit was gone, and some others have seen him, most of them women when their husbands are away. Missus Burt Williams said he was tied to her corral for three or four hours one day."

"But surely someone has seen the rider come and mount up?"

"Never. He'll be out there like he is now . . . wait! . . . he's gone!"

Kedrick came to his feet with a start and stared out the door. Sue was right. The mouse-colored horse was gone. His own Appaloosa stood where he had been left, but the grulla had disappeared.

Walking out into the yard, he looked around very carefully, but there was nothing in sight on the plain or the hills. The horse—and he was positive he had seen it only a few minutes before—was gone! He looked at her and saw the strained expression on her face, then he walked out to the Appaloosa. Pinned to his saddle was a note. He took it down and glanced at it, then passed it to Sue who had come up beside him.

Stay away

Kedrick shrugged. "Your brother do this?"

"Oh, no! I told him about the horse and he knew no more about it than I. Besides, he didn't print that. He couldn't. Pit never learned either to read or write."

Long after he left the Malpais Arroyo behind, he was puzzling over the strange horse. Somebody was seriously trying either to puzzle or frighten the squatters, yet it was an action unlike the company. Moreover, it must be somebody who had a lot of time to spend.

Kedrick rode north toward Blue Hill, then swung out, crossing the old Mormon Trail and skirting the rim. This was good grazing land. There was an abundance of rough foliage here and a good herd of cattle could fatten on this range without trouble. Moreover, the herding problem was solved in part by the rim that provided a natural drift fence beyond which the cattle could not go. When he reached Salt Creek, he turned down the creek toward the river, but swung east again, and, passing near Chimney Rock, he rode southeast until he struck the Hogback Trail. Once over that ridge he headed due east for Mustang.

Yet, as always, his eyes were alive and alert. He loved this land, harsh though it might be at times. He loved the dim purples and blues, the far-flung mists and mornings and nights, the gray-green of the sagebrush, and the rust-red of the sandstone. It was a good country, and there was room for all if it were left open for settlement.

His own mind was not yet resolved. The problem of his debt to Gunter weighed heavily upon him, and there were other considerations. He wanted no trouble, and to withdraw now might mean plenty of it, particularly if he remained in the country, which he had every reason to do. He would try to talk the company into withdrawing, but knew that would fail.

Just where, in all this, did Connie Duane actually stand? Was she involved more deeply than he believed? Or was it only what had been implied, that her uncle had invested her money in the land speculation? If such was the case, it might be difficult or impossible to get out at this stage—even if they would allow it. Burwick puzzled him. Obviously the controlling power, he gave no evidence of where that power came from, aside from some native shrewdness. Yet there might be much more to the man and evidently was, for that Keith and Gunter deferred to him was obvious. Purposely Kedrick had said nothing of his hideaway near Yellow Butte when talking to Sue. That young lady already knew

142

more than was good for her, and that spot might again become useful. It was something to know.

Mustang was asleep when he rode into the town and headed for the stable. He put his horse up and rubbed it down thoroughly, gave it a good bait of corn, and forked down some hay. Then he made his way quickly to the St. James. As he neared the hotel, a tall, lean figure arose from the chair where he himself had been sitting a few days before. The build and the broad hat, the very hang of the guns left no mistake. It was Laredo Shad.

"Cap'n?" The voice was low. "You all right?"

"Yes, and you?"

Shad chuckled. "Don't worry none about Shad! I stay healthy." He motioned to a chair. "You better sit down. I've been hopin' you'd show up."

"What's the talk? Did they think I was dead, or skipped the country?"

"Some o' both, I reckon. Keith was fit to be tied. He wants to see you as soon as you show . . . no matter when."

"He'll wait. I'm tired."

Shad nodded, then lighted his cigarette, which had gone out. "You know, I ain't right sure about this business."

Kedrick nodded. "I know what you mean. I'm not the man to run folks out of their homes."

"You quittin'?"

"Not yet. I'll talk to 'em first."

143

"Won't do no good. They are mighty blood-thirsty. It was Poinsett shot that messenger. Dornie put him up to it. Poinsett killed him, an' then four, five of those rannies shot up the body. I don't think Fessenden shot any, an' maybe Goff didn't. You can lay your last *peso* I didn't shoot none. It was mighty raw, Cap'n, mighty raw."

"They'll pay for it. Were you on the Yellow Butte raid?"

"Uh-huh, but I didn't shoot nobody. I'm no Bible packer, Cap'n, but I do figure a fightin' man shouldn't tackle folks who cain't fight back, an' I ain't the man to be firin' on no women or kids."

"What are they talkin' up now? Any plans you know of?"

Shad hesitated, then shrugged. "Reckon you'd better talk that out with them, Cap'n. I may know somethin', but I ain't tellin', not yet."

The Texan sat silently for a few minutes while both men smoked, and then he waved an impatient hand. "Cap'n, I hired on as a gun hand, an' such I am, but I didn't figure on this sort of thing. Some of those *hombres* on the other side o' this shindig look a damned sight more human than some on our own side. I'm gettin' shut o' the whole shebang."

"Uh-huh"—surprisingly Kedrick found reso-lution coming to him—"I know how you feel, but my own way will be different. I think, if I can't talk Gunter an' the rest of them out of it, I'll change sides."

Shad nodded. "I've thought of it. I sure have."

Kedrick turned suddenly and found Dornie Shaw standing not twenty feet behind them. Slowly he got to his feet, and Laredo Shad did likewise. Shaw's eyes avoided Kedrick. "If you figure on leavin' us, Shad, you better figure on killin' me first."

"If I have to," Laredo said quietly, "then I reckon you can die as simple as any other man. Want to try it now?"

"That's enough, Shad!" Kedrick's voice was sharp. "I've said there would be no more fighting. Not in this outfit."

Dornie Shaw turned his head slowly and smiled at Kedrick. "Still like to give orders, do you? Maybe that'll be changed."

"Maybe." Tom Kedrick shrugged. "That will be time enough for me to stop giving orders. I'm turning in."

"Keith wants to see you."

"He can wait. I've had a rough time. There's nothing he wants won't wait."

"Shall I tell him that?"

"If you like."

Shaw smiled again. "You must carry a lot o' weight where you come from, Kedrick, but don't forget it ain't here. Keith is a bad man to buck. So's Burwick."

145

Kedrick shrugged again. "I've bucked worse. But at the moment I'm bucking nobody. I need sleep, and, by the Lord Harry, sleep is what I'll get. Whatever Keith has on his mind can wait until daylight. I'll be up then."

Shaw started to go, then hesitated, unable to restrain his curiosity. "What happened to you? We figured you were dead or taken prisoner when you didn't come back."

For the first time Kedrick began to wonder. Had Shaw wanted the messenger killed for that very reason? Had he deliberately moved that way hoping the enraged settlers would kill Kedrick? It was most likely. "It doesn't matter," he said, passing off the remark casually. "I found a way to keep out of sight."

Shaw turned away, and, when he had gone only a few steps, Tom Kedrick spoke up suddenly: "By the way, Dornie. Know anybody who rides a grulla mustang?"

Shaw stopped abruptly, but he did not turn. His whole body seemed to stiffen. Then he started on. "No," he said gruffly, "I sure don't."

Laredo Shad stared after him. "You know, pardner, you'll either kill that *hombre* someday or you'll be killed."

"Uh-huh," Kedrick said quietly, "I've the same feeling."

VII

Keith was pacing the floor in the office at the gray stone building when Kedrick walked in. He stopped and turned swiftly. "Shaw tells me you came in after midnight. Why didn't you come to me according to my orders?"

"Frankly I was tired. Furthermore"—Kedrick returned Keith's look—"I'd nothing to report that wouldn't keep."

"You were hired to do a job, and you haven't done it." Keith stood with his hands on his hips. "Where've you been?"

Briefly and clearly Kedrick explained, omitting only the visit to Laines' and the story of the hide-out. He continued: "Having looked the situation over, I'd say you had small chance of driving those people off. Also, you and Gunter misrepresented things to me and the government. That land is occupied not by renegades and outlaws, but by good, solid people. You can't get away with running them off."

Keith smiled contemptuously. "Getting scared? You were supposed to be a fighting man. As for what we can do or can't do, let me tell you this, Kedrick. We've started to run those people off, and we'll do it. With or without you! Hiring you was Gunter's idea, anyway."

"That's right, it was." Gunter walked into the room followed by Burwick, and he glanced swiftly from Kedrick to Keith. "If you're complainin' about his going to look over that country, you can stop. I sent him."

"Did you tell him to come back scared to death? Saying we can't swing it?"

Burwick had been silent, but now he moved to the big chair behind the desk and dropped into it. He sighed heavily and wiped the back of his hand across his mouth, then glanced at Kedrick keenly. "What did you find out?"

"That they are determined to fight. I talked to Bob McLennon and to Slagle. There's no quit in those men. They'll fight at the drop of a hat, and to the last ditch. Right now, at this minute, they are ready for anything. Your raid killed one man, wounded another. The dynamite blasted a door loose and blew a hole in the porch."

Burwick turned swiftly and glared at Keith. "You told me three men dead and a building destroyed! Hereafter, you be sure reports to me are accurate." He swung back to Kedrick. "Go on, what happened to you? You got away?"

"I'm here."

Their eyes met and held for a long time, Burwick's stone-cold and hard, examining, probing.

"What do you think of the deal?" he asked finally.

"The fight," Kedrick replied carefully, "will raise a stink clear to Washington. Remember the Lincoln County War? We'll have us another general down here, and you know how much profit you'll make out of that place then!"

Burwick nodded his huge head. "Sensible, that's sensible. Have to think our way around that. At least"—he glared again at Keith and Gunter—"this man can bring in some sensible ideas and make a coherent report. You two could learn from him." He looked up at Kedrick. "Anything else?"

"A couple of things. There's a mysterious rider out on those plains. Rides a mouse-colored horse, and he's got those folks more jittery than all your threats."

Burwick was uninterested. He shuffled papers on his desk. "What's this I hear about you quittin'?"

"I won't be a party to murder. These people aren't outlaws, but good, substantial folks. I'd say buy them out or leave them alone."

"You aren't running this affair," Keith replied coldly. "We will decide what is to be done."

"Nobody quits," Burwick said quietly, his eyes on Kedrick, "unless I say so."

Tom Kedrick smiled suddenly. "Then you'd better say so, because I've quit as of now!"

"Tom!" Gunter protested. "Let's talk this over!"

"What of the money you owe the firm?" Keith

149

demanded unpleasantly. "You can repay that, I suppose?"

"There's no need." Connie Duane stood in the doorway. They all turned at the sound of her voice.

They all turned at the voice. Connie Duane stood in the door. "You have money of mine in this project. When Uncle John got it from me, he told me it was a real estate speculation. His other activities have been honest and practical, so I did not investigate. Now I have. I shall withdraw my money, and you can pay me less the sum advanced to Captain Kedrick. He may repay me when circumstances permit it."

All in the room were still. Gunter's face was pale, and Keith looked startled, then angry. He started to protest, but he was too slow. Burwick turned on Gunter. "You!" he snorted angrily. "You told me that was your money! You fool! What do you mean, bringing a woman into a deal like this? Well, you brought her in. Now you manage her or I shall!"

"Nobody," Connie replied, "is managing me or my affairs from now on. I'll handle them myself!" She turned to Kedrick. "I'm glad, Captain, that you've made this decision. I am sure you'll not be sorry for it."

Kedrick turned to follow her from the room, but Burwick's voice stopped him. "Captain!"

He turned. Keith's eyes were ugly and Gunter's

face was haunted by doubt and fear. "Captain Kedrick," Burwick said, "I believe we are all being too hasty. I like your caution in this matter. Your suggestion that cleaning out those people might make trouble and cause talk in Washington is probable. I had considered that but, not knowing McLennon, had considered the chance negligible. Slagle, I know. McLennon I do not know. Your suggestion eliminates a frontal attack. We must try some other means. Also," he added, "I believe that your presence has some claim on that of Miss Duane. Consequently, as we can brook no failure now, I have a proposition for you. How would you like to come into the firm? As a silent partner?"

Keith's face flushed angrily, but Gunter looked up, his eyes suddenly hopeful. Burwick continued: "We could give you a fifteen percent interest, which, believe me, will be adequate. I believe you could keep Miss Duane in line, and with you at the helm we might straighten this whole thing out . . . without bloodshed."

Kedrick hesitated. The money was a temptation, for he had no desire to be indebted to Connie, yet the money alone would mean nothing. It was that last phrase that gripped his attention and made him incautious. "Without bloodshed," he repeated. "On those terms, I accept. However, let's discuss this matter a bit further."

Keith spun on his heel. "Burwick, this doesn't

make sense! You know the only way we'll get these people off is by driving them off! We agreed on that before. Also, this man is not reliable. I happen to know that he has friends on the other side, and has actually been in communication with them."

"So much the better." Burwick pursed his fat lips and mopped perspiration from his face. "He'll have a contact he can use then to make a deal." He chuckled. "Suppose you two run along and let me talk to Captain Kedrick?"

Hours later, Tom Kedrick paused on the street and studied it with care. Burwick had been more than reasonable, little as he was able to trust him, yet he thought it possible that Burwick was sincere in his agreement to buy off a few of them, and to try to convince others. Certainly, if the government moved in, they would have to move, anyway. With McLennon and Slagle out of the picture the chances were there would be no fight, for the others lacked leadership. No fighting meant no deaths, and the settlers would come out of it with a little money at least.

He paced the street irritably, avoiding company. Burwick stank of deceit, but the man was practical and he should realize that a sudden mess of killings preceding the sale of the land would create a furor that might cause them to lose out all around. At least trouble had been avoided for the time, and even Connie was hopeful that something might be done. Tomorrow he was returning again to try to make some deal with McLennon and Slagle. A neutral messenger was leaving tonight.

"They won't come to town," Burwick had agreed, "so why not pick some intermediate point? Meet them, say, at Largo Cañon or Chimney Rock? Have your talk there, and I'll come with you. Just you and me, McLennon and Slagle. We can talk there and maybe make peace. Ain't it worth a try?"

It was only that chance for peace that had persuaded him and helped him to persuade Connie. She had listened in silence as he explained the situation, then she had turned to him frankly. "Captain, you don't trust them, and neither do I. Uncle John has never been this way before, and I believe somehow he has fallen under the domination of those other men. However, I think that, if Burwick is willing to talk, we should at least agree. I'll stand by you in this, and we'll hope something can come of it that will prevent trouble."

Kedrick was less hopeful than he had let it appear, and now he was studying the situation from every angle. As things stood, it was a stale-mate. He was confident that with McLennon and Slagle to lead them, the settlers could manage a stiff defense of their town and their homes.

Certainly they could prevent the survey being completed and prevent any use being made of the lands. Yet there were fiery elements on both sides, and Keith did not like the turn things had taken. Colonel Loren Keith had from the very beginning planned on striking fast and wiping out the opposition. It would be merely another unsolved mystery of the West. Kedrick resolved to keep an eye on the man and be prepared for anything.

He returned to the St. James and to bed, yet he awakened early and was surprised to see Keith, mounted and riding out of town at daybreak. With a bound he was out of bed and dressing. Whatever Keith had in mind he meant to know. Swiftly he descended the stairs and went to the livery stable. Mounted, he headed out of town, found Keith's tracks with ease, and followed them. Keith turned off the trail and headed west and slightly north, but after a few miles Kedrick lost the trail and took a wide swing to try and cut it again, but Keith had vanished somewhere in the vicinity of Largo Cañon.

Returning to the hotel, he found a message from Bob McLennon. He and Slagle would meet with Burwick and Kedrick at Chimney Rock at three in the afternoon on Wednesday. It was now Monday, and a whole day lay between. Yet during the remainder of Monday he saw nothing of Dornie Shaw, although Laredo Shad appeared a couple of times, then vanished into one of the saloons.

At midnight the door of his room opened slowly and Tom Kedrick sat up, gun in hand. It was Laredo Shad.

"Somethin's up," he said, dropping on the bed, "an' she looks mighty peculiar. Couple of hours ago Poinsett an' Goff showed up an' said they had quit. No fightin' here, so they were pullin' out for Durango. About a half hour later, they mounted up an' took off."

"What's peculiar about that?" Kedrick inquired, building a smoke. "That's in line with Burwick's talk with me."

"Yeah," Shad replied dryly, "but both of them came in here with a good deal of gear. They lost their pack horses somewheres and went out only with what they could carry on the one horse, an' damned little o' that."

"What about Fessenden?"

"Ain't seen him."

"Any of the others gone?"

"Clauson is. At least he ain't around in sight. I ain't seen him since morning."

That left Shaw, who had been around little himself, and Fessenden if he was still in town. Despite himself, Kedrick was disturbed, but if Burwick was getting rid of his warriors, it was a good sign, and probably, Kedrick felt, he was getting too suspicious. Nothing, Shad said, had been said to him about quitting. "In fact," Shad said dryly, "the Mixus boys pulled in this morning, an' they went right to Burwick."

"Who are they?"

"Killers. Dry-gulchers, mostly. Bean an' Abe Mixus. They were in that Sandoval affair. Couple of men died awful opportune in that affair, an', come to think of it, Burwick was around. Fact is, that was where I met him."

"Were you in that?"

"Uh-huh. I was in town, though, an' had me a run-in with Roy Gangle. Roy was a mighty tough ranny who'd been ramroddin' a big spread down thataway, an', when he got into the war, he went bad, plumb bad. We'd had trouble over a steer, an' he braced me. He was a mite slow."

It made no sense—gunmen leaving, but others arriving. Of course, the Mixus boys could have been spoken to before the change of plans. That must be it. He suggested as much to Laredo, and the Texan nodded dubiously. "Maybe. I don't trust that *hombre* none. Your man Gunter is in over his head. Keith, well, he's all around bad when it comes to that, but neither of them can hold a candle to that Burwick."

Study the situation as he could, Tom Kedrick could see no answer to it, and the fact remained that they were to meet Slagle and McLennon for a peace conference. Out of that anything might come, and he had no real cause to distrust Burwick. Morning was bright and clear with the sun promising a hot day. Yet it was still cool when Kedrick appeared on the street and crossed to the little restaurant where he ate in silence. He was on his second cup of coffee when Connie came in.

Her face brightened with a smile as she saw him, and she came over to his table. "You know, you're the one bright spot in this place. I'm so tired of that old stone house and seeing that dirty old man around that I can scarcely stand it. I'll be glad when this is all over."

He studied her. "What will you do then?"

"You know, I've not really thought of that. What I want to do is to get a ranch somewhere, a place with trees, grass, and some running water. It doesn't have to be a big place."

"Cattle?"

"A few, but horses are what I want. Horses like that one of yours, I think."

"Good idea. It takes less land for horses, and there's always a market for good stock." He studied the beauty of her mouth, the quietness and humor of her eyes. "Somehow I'm glad to think you're staying. It wouldn't be the same without you. Not now."

She looked at him quickly, her eyes dancing with laughter, but with the hint of a question in their depths. "Why, Tom! That sounds almost like gallantry. Like you were trying to make love to me, like all the cowboys."

"No, Connie," he said quietly, "when I make love to you, there won't be any doubt about it. You'll know, and I won't be fooling. Over west of here, west and south, there's a great rim that stretches for miles across the country, and a splendid pine forest atop it. There's trees, water, game, and some of the finest mountain meadows a man ever saw. I know a place over there where I camped once, a good spring, some tall trees, graceful in the wind, and a long sweep of land clear to the rim's edge, and beyond it miles upon miles of rolling, sweeping range and forest."

"It sounds fascinating, like what I've been wanting ever since I came West."

He pushed back his chair and stood up. "Maybe when this is over, you'd ride over that way with me? I'd like to show it to you."

She looked up at him. "All right, Tom. We'll look at it together."

He paused, hat in hand, staring out the door. "Together," he mused. Then he glanced down at her. "You know, Connie, that's the most beautiful word in the language . . . together."

He walked away then, pausing to pay his check and hers, before stepping outside into the warmth of the street. A buckboard had stopped and a man was getting out of it, a man who moved warily and looked half frightened. He glanced around swiftly, then ducked through the door into the store.

VIII

Two men crossed the street suddenly. One of them was a man Kedrick had never seen before; the other was the sly-looking loafer he had seen hanging around the back door in the saloon at Yellow Butte. The loafer, a sour-faced man called Singer, was talking. They stopped, and he indicated the buckboard to the man with him. "That's him, Abe," Singer was saying, "he's one of that crowd from across the way. He's brother-in-law to McLennon."

"This is a good place to start," Abe replied shortly, low-voiced. "Let's go!"

Tom Kedrick turned on his heel and followed them. As they stepped into the door, he stepped after and caught it before it slammed shut. Neither man seemed to be aware of his presence, for they were intent on the man at the counter.

"Hello, Sloan," Singer said softly. "Meet Abe Mixus."

The name must have meant something to Sloan, for he turned, his face gray. He held a baby's bottle that he was in the act of buying in his right hand. His eyes, quick and terror-stricken, went from one to the other. He was frightened, and puzzled, and he seemed to be fighting for self-control. "You in this squabble, Singer? I figured you to be outside of it."

Singer chuckled. "That's what I aim for folks to think."

Mixus, a lean, stooped man with yellow eye-balls and a thin-cheeked face, drew a paper from his pocket. "That's a quit-claim deed, Sloan," he said. "You can sign it an' save yourself trouble."

Sloan's eyes went to the deed and seemed to hold there, then, slowly, they lifted. "I can't do that. My wife's having a child in the next couple of days. I worked too hard on that place to give it up. I reckon I can't sign."

"I say you better." Mixus's voice was cold, level. The storekeeper had vanished, and the room was empty save for the three, and for Tom Kedrick, standing in the shadows near some hanging jeans and slickers. "I say you better sign because you don't own that prop'ty anyhow. Want to call me a liar?"

Resolution seemed to have overcome Sloan's immediate fear. He was a brave man, and Kedrick knew that whatever he said now, he would die. He spoke first.

"No, Abe," he said softly, "I'll call you a liar."

Mixus stiffened as if struck. He was a killer, and dangerous, but he was a smart, sure-thing killer, and he had believed himself alone but for Singer. Now somebody was behind him. He stood stock-still, then started to turn. Singer had fallen back against the wall, his eyes starting to locate Kedrick.

"It's Kedrick," he said. "The boss gunman."

Mixus scowled. "What's the matter?" he said irritably. "What yuh buttin' in for?"

"There's to be no more killing, Abe." Kedrick held his ground. "We're havin' a peace conference tomorrow. This killing is over."

"Got my orders," Mixus persisted. "You talk to Burwick." There was a movement from Sloan, and he whirled on him. "You stand still!" he barked.

"You can go, Sloan," Kedrick said. "Get in your outfit an' tell McLennon that my word is good. You'd better stop thinking about him, Abe. You're in trouble, and I'm the trouble."

Mixus was confused. He knew Kedrick was ramrodding the gunmen for the company, and he was puzzled. Had he been about to do the wrong thing? But, no, he hadn't. "You fool!" His confusion burst into fury. "Keith tol' me to git him!"

"Shut up!" Singer yelled. "Damn it! You . . ."

Abe Mixus was a cold-blooded killer and no heavyweight mentally. Orders and counterorders had come to him and, worked up to such a killing pitch, he had been suddenly stopped in the middle of it and switched off into this back trail where he floundered hopelessly. Now Singer seemed to be turning on him, and he swung toward him, his teeth bared, his face vicious.

"Don't you tell me, you white-livered coyote!" he snarled.

One hand hung over a gun, and Singer, frightened, grabbed for his own gun. Instantly Mixus whipped out his .44 and flame stabbed at Singer. The renegade turned on his heel. His knees slowly buckled and he slid to the floor, his head against a sack of flour, blood welling from his mouth.

Mixus stared down at him, and then, slowly, he blinked, then blinked again. Awareness seemed to return to him, and his jittery nerves calmed. He stared down at Singer almost unbelieving. "Why, I . . . I . . . kilt Singer," he said.

"That's right." Kedrick was watching him, knowing now upon what a slender thread of irritation this man's muscles were poised. "What will Keith say to that?"

Cunning came over Abe's horse-like face. "Keith? What give you the idee he had anythin' to do with this?" he demanded.

Slowly, attracted by the shooting and made confident by its end, people were gathering in front of the door. The storekeeper had come into the room and stood watching, his face drawn and frightened.

Tom Kedrick took a slow step back as Abe's eyes turned toward the front of the store. Putting the slickers between them, he moved on cat feet to the opening between the counters and slid through into the living quarters and out into the alley behind the store.

Crossing the street below the crowd, he wound up in front of the St. James, pausing there. Laredo Shad materialized beside him. "What happened?" he asked swiftly.

Kedrick explained. "I don't get it," he said. "Keith may be moving on his own, but Burwick was to hold off until we had our talk . . . and I know Keith didn't like that. He spoke right up about it."

"Ain't Singer supposed to be a settler?" Shad asked. "Won't this serve to get 'em all riled up? Who knew that Singer was with Keith an' the company?"

"You've got a point there," Kedrick said thoughtfully. "This may be the very thing that will blow the lid off. Both of them were mighty jumpy. It looked like they had Sloan marked because he was McLennon's relative. I sprung a surprise on them, an' Mixus just couldn't get himself located."

The crowd separated, then gathered in knots along the street to discuss the new event. Shad loitered there beside him, and was standing there when Loren Keith came up. He glanced sharply at Shad, then at Kedrick. "What's happened over there?"

He kept his eyes on Kedrick as he spoke, and Kedrick shrugged. "Shooting, I guess. Not unusual for Mustang from what I hear."

"Mixus was in there," Shad commented. "Wonder if he had a hand in it?"

Keith turned and looked at Laredo, suspicion in his eyes. "Who was shot?" he inquired, his eyes going from one to the other.

"Singer, they tell me," Shad said casually. "I reckon Mixus killed him."

"Mixus? Killed Singer?" Keith shook his head. "That's preposterous!"

"Don't know why," Laredo drawled. "Mixus come heah to fight, didn't he? An' ain't Singer one o' them settlers?"

Colonel Keith hesitated, his sharp, hard features a picture of doubt and uncertainty. Watching him, Kedrick was amused and pleased. The store-keeper had not seen him, and it was doubtful if anyone had but Mixus, the dead man, and the now missing Sloan.

What Abe Mixus would offer as an explanation for shooting Singer, Tom couldn't conceive, but a traitor had died, and the enemy was confounded. Little as it might mean in the long run, it was for the moment a good thing. The only fly in the ointment was the fact that Singer had been a squatter, and that few if any knew of his tie-up with Keith and the company.

Watching the crowds in the street, Tom Kedrick began to perceive a new element shaping itself. Public opinion was a force Burwick had not reckoned with, and the faces of the men talking in the streets were hard and bitter. These were mostly poor men who had made their own way or were engaged in making their way, and they resented the action of the company. Few had known Singer well, and those few had little use for the man, but the issue, from their viewpoint, was not a matter of personalities, but a matter of a bunch of hard-working men against the company, an organization largely of outsiders, seeking to profit from the work of local people. Furthermore, whatever Singer was, he was not a gunman and he was a local man. Abe Mixus was a known killer, a gunman whose gun was for hire.

Tom Kedrick nodded toward the street. "Well, Colonel," he said, "you'd better start thinking about that, unless you want to stretch hemp. That bunch is sore."

Keith stared at them nervously, then nodded and hurried away toward headquarters. Shad watched him go, and turned toward Kedrick. "You know, we're sort of tied in with the company, an' I don't want to hang for 'em. Let's light a shuck out of here an' stick in the hills for a few days?"

"Can't. I've got to make that meeting with Burwick. But you might get out of town, anyway.

Scout around and see what you can find of Goff and them . . . if they really left the country or not. Meet me at Chimney Rock about five tomorrow evening . . . make it later . . . about sundown."

Leaving Shad, Kedrick hurried to his room in the St. James and bundled his gear together. He carried it down to the livery stable and saddled the Appaloosa. When that was done, he headed for headquarters, staying off the main street. Yet it was Connie Duane he wanted to see, and not Burwick or Keith.

There was no sign of any of them. Gunter was not around, and Burwick and Keith seemed to have vanished. Idling in the office, Tom heard a slight movement upstairs. He called out. Feet hurried along the floor above him, and then Connie was at the stair head. "Yes?" Recognizing him, she hurried down. "Is something wrong?"

Swiftly he explained, not holding anything back. "Nothing may come of it, although it wouldn't take much to start it, and they all know that the company gunmen are mostly out of town. Burwick, Keith, and your uncle must have lit out."

"Uncle John hasn't been around all day. I saw him at breakfast, and then he disappeared."

"I'll look around. Do you have a gun?" He shook his head then. "Don't much think you'll need it, most of them like you around here, and you've been pretty outspoken. But stay close

166

to your room. The lid's going to blow off."

He turned away, but she called to him: "Tom?" He turned when he reached the door. He seemed to see pleading in her eyes. "Be careful, Tom"

Their eyes held for a long moment, and then he nodded. "I will if I . . . can."

He went out and paused on the steps. Burwick and Keith might get out of the way, but whatever else Gunter might be, he was scarcely the man to leave his niece behind at a time of danger. Puzzled that he should be this inconsistent, Kedrick paused and looked around him. The back street was bare and empty. The white, powdery dust lay thickly and had sifted into the foliage of the trees and shrubs.

Kedrick hitched his guns into place and walked slowly around the house. The stable lay behind it, but it was usually filled with horses. Now it seemed empty. He strode back, his spurs jingling a little and tiny puffs of dust rising from his boots as he walked. Once, nearly to the stable, he paused by a water trough and listened for noise from the town. It was quiet, altogether too quiet. He hesitated, worrying about Connie again, but then went on and into the wide door that gave entrance to the shadowed coolness of the stable.

The stalls were empty, all save one. He walked back, then paused. The chestnut was Gunter's horse, and his saddle lay nearby. Could he be somewhere around town? Kedrick considered that, then dismissed it. He removed his hat and wiped the band with his kerchief, then replaced it. His face was unusually thoughtful, and he walked to the far end of the stable, examining every stall as he walked back.

Nothing.

Puzzled, he stepped out into the bright glare of the sun, and heard no sound anywhere. He squinted his eyes around, then saw the ramshackle old building that had done duty for a stable before the present large one was built. He stared at it, and then turned in that direction. He had taken scarcely a step when he heard a rattle of hoofs, and swung swiftly around, half crouched, his hands wide.

Then he straightened. Sue Laine slid from her horse and ran to him. "Oh, I've found you, Tom!" she cried, catching him by the arms. "Tom, don't go to that meeting tomorrow. There's going to be trouble!"

"You mean, McLennon's framed something?"

"McLennon?" For an instant she was startled. "Oh, no! Not Mac!" Her expression changed. "Come home with me, Tom. Please do! Let them have this out and get it over with! Come home with me!"

"Why all this sudden worry about me?" He was sincerely puzzled. "We've met only once, and we seem to have different ideas about things."

"Don't stand there and argue! Tom, I mustn't be

seen talking to you . . . not by either side. Come with me and get away from here until this is all over. I've seen Dornie, and he hates you, Tom. He hates you."

"He does, does he?" He patted her arm. "Run along home now. I've things to do here."

"Oh?" Her eyes hardened a little. "Is it that woman? That Duane girl? I've heard all about her, how beautiful she is, how . . . how she . . . what kind of girl is she?"

"She's a lovely person," he said gravely. "You'd like her, Sue."

Sue stiffened. "Would I? I wonder how much you know about women, Tom? Or do you know anything about them? I could never like Connie Duane!" She shook his arm. "Come, if you're coming. I just heard this last night, and I can't . . . I won't see this happen."

"What? What's going to happen?"

She stamped her foot with impatience. "Oh, you fool, you! They plan to kill you, Tom! Now, come on!"

"Not now," he said quietly. "I've got to get this fight settled first, then maybe I'll ride your way. Now run along. I've got to look around."

Impatiently she turned and walked to her horse. In the saddle she glanced back at him. "If you change your mind . . ."

"Not now," he repeated.

"Then be careful. Be careful, Tom."

He watched her go, then happened to glance toward the house. Connie Duane stood in the window, looking down at him, but as he looked up, she turned sharply away. He started for the house, then hesitated. There was nothing he could say now, nothing that would have any effect or do any good at all.

He started toward the front of the house again, then stopped. On an impulse he turned and walked swiftly back to the little old building and caught the latch. The door was weathered and gray. It creaked on rusty hinges and opened rheumatically. Inside, there was the musty odor of decay. Kedrick stood there for a minute watching the sunlight filter through the cobwebbed window and fall in a faint square upon the ancient straw that littered the earthen floor, and then he stepped forward, peering around the corner of the nearest stall.

John Gunter lay sprawled upon his face, his head pillowed upon one forearm, the back of his shirt covered with a dark, wide stain. Kedrick knelt beside him.

Connie's uncle had been stabbed in the back. Three powerful blows, from the look of the wounds, had been struck downward—evidently while he sat at a desk or table. He had been dead for several hours.

IX

Alton Burwick, for all his weight, sat his saddle easily and rode well. His horse was a blood bay, tall and long-limbed. He walked it alongside Tom Kedrick's Appaloosa, and from time to time he spurred it to a trot, then eased down. On this morning Burwick wore an ancient gray felt hat, torn at the flat crown, and a soiled handkerchief that concealed his greasy shirt collar. His shirt bulged over his belt, and he wore one gun, too high on his hip for easy use. His whiskers seemed neither to have grown nor been clipped. They were still a rough stubble of dirty, mixed gray. Yet he seemed unusually genial this morning.

"Great country, Kedrick! Country for a man to live in! If this deal goes through, you should get yourself a ranch. I aim to."

"Not a bad idea." Kedrick rode with his right hand dangling. "I was talking about that yesterday, with Connie Duane."

The smile vanished from Burwick's face. "You talked to her yesterday? What time?"

"Afternoon." Kedrick let his voice become casual, yet he was alert to the change in Burwick's voice. Had Burwick murdered Gunter? Or had it been one of the squatters? With things as they were, it would be difficult or impossible to prove. "We had a long talk. She's a fine girl."

Burwick said nothing, but his lips tightened. The red cañon walls lifted high above them, for along here they were nearly five hundred feet above the bottom of Salt Creek. There was but little farther to go, he knew, and he was puzzled by Burwick's increased watchfulness. The man might suspect treachery, but he had said nothing to imply anything of the kind.

Tom's mind reverted to Sue's warning of the previous day—they intended to kill him—but who were "they"? She had not been specific in her warning except to say that he should not keep this rendezvous today. Kedrick turned the idea over in his mind, wondering if she were deliberately trying to prevent a settlement, or if she knew something and was genuinely worried.

Pit Laine, her gun-slinging brother, was one element in the situation he could not estimate. Laine had not been mentioned in any of the discussions and he seemed always just beyond reach, just out of sight, yet definitely in the background as was the mysterious rider of the mouse-colored horse. That whole story seemed fantastic, but Kedrick did not think Sue was inclined to fall for tall stories.

The cañon of Salt Creek widened out and several branch cañons opened into it. They left the creek bed and rode closer together to the towering cliffs, now all of seven hundred feet above the trail. They were heading south, and Burwick, mopping his sweating face from time to time with a dirty handkerchief, was no longer talking. Kedrick pushed back his hat and rolled a smoke. He had never seen Burwick so jittery before, and he was puzzled. Deliberately he had said nothing to any of the company about Gunter, although he had arranged with some of the townspeople to have the body moved. Tom was afraid it might precipitate the very trouble he was trying to end, and bring the fight into open battle. Moreover, he was not at all sure of why Gunter had been killed, or who had done it. That it could be retaliation for Singer's death was an answer to be considered, but it might have been done by either Keith or Burwick.

He drew up suddenly, for a horse had left recent tracks coming in alone from the northwest. Burwick followed his eyes, studying the tracks. "I've seen those tracks before," Tom Kedrick said. "Now whose horse is that?"

"We better step it up," Burwick said impatiently. "They'll be there before us."

They pushed on into the bright, still morning. The sky overhead was a vast blue dome scattered with fleecy puffballs of clouds, like bolts of cotton on the surface of a lake of pure blue. The red cliffs towered high on their left, and the valley on their right swept away in a vast, gently rolling panorama. Glancing off over this sagebrush-dotted valley, Tom knew that lost in the blue haze, some seven or eight miles away, was Malpais Arroyo and Sue Laine. Was she there this morning? Or was she riding somewhere? She was strangely attractive, that slim, dark-haired, dark-eyed girl with her lovely skin, soft despite the desert sun and desert wind. She had come to him, riding all that distance to bring him a warning of danger. Why? Was it simply that she feared for him? Was she in love with him? He dismissed that idea instantly, but continued to wonder. She was, despite her beauty, a hard, calculating girl, hating the country around, and wanting only to be free of it.

Heat waves danced out over the bottomland, and shadows gathered under the red wall. A dust devil lifted and danced weirdly across the desert, then lost itself among the thick antelope brush and the catclaw. Tom Kedrick mopped his brow and swung his horse farther east, the tall spire of Chimney Rock lifting in the distance, its heavier shouldered companion looming beside and beyond it.

"Look!" Burwick's voice held a note of triumph. "There they come!"

To the south, and still three or four miles off, they could see two riders heading toward Chimney Rock. At this distance they could not be distinguished, but their destination was obvious.

"Now that's fine!" Burwick beamed. "They'll

174

be here right on time! Say"—he glanced at his heavy gold watch—"tell you what. You'll be there a shade before them, so what say you wait for them while I have me a look at a ledge up in the cañon?"

In the shadow of the rock, Kedrick swung down. There was a small pool of water there. He let the Appaloosa drink and ground-hitched him deeper in the shade, near some grass. Then he walked back and, dropping to the ground, lit a smoke. He could see the two riders nearing now. One was on a fast-stepping chestnut, the other a dappled gray.

They rode up and swung down. The first man was Pete Slagle, the second a stranger who Kedrick had not seen before. "Where's McLennon?" he asked.

"He'll be along. He hadn't come in from the ranch, so I came on with Steelman here. He's a good man, an' anything he says goes with all of us. Bob'll be along later, though, if you have to have his word."

"Burwick came. He's over lookin' at a ledge he saw in the cañon over there."

The three men bunched and Steelman studied Kedrick. "Dai Reid tells me you're a good man . . . trustworthy, he says."

"I aim to be." He drew a last drag on his cigarette and lifted his head to snap it out into the sand. For an instant he stood poised, his face blank, then realization hit him. "Look out!" he yelled. "Hit the dirt!"

His voice was drowned in a roar of guns and something smashed him in the body even as he fell, then something else slugged him atop the head and a vast wave of blackness folded over him, pushing him down, down, down, deeper and deeper into a swirling darkness that closed in tightly around his body, around his throat. And then there was nothing, nothing at all.

Alton Burwick smiled and threw down his cigar. Calmly he swung into the saddle and rode toward the four men who were riding from behind a low parapet of rocks near Chimney Rock. As he rode up, they were standing, rifles in hand, staring toward the cluster of bloody figures sprawled on the ground in the shade. "Got 'em!" Shaw said. His eyes were hard. "That cleans it up, an' good!"

Fessenden, Clauson, and Poinsett stared at the bodies, saying nothing. Lee Goff walked toward them from his vantage point where he had awaited anyone who might have had a chance to escape. He stooped over the three.

Slagle was literally riddled with bullets, his body smashed and bloody. Off to one side lay Steelman, half the top of his head blown off. Captain Kedrick lay sprawled deeper in the shadow, his head bloody, and a dark stain on his body.

"Want I should finish 'em off for sure?" Poinsett asked.

"Finish what off?" Clauson sneered. "Look at 'em . . . shot to doll rags."

"What about Kedrick?" Fessenden asked. "He dead for sure?"

"Deader'n Columbus," Goff said.

"Hey!" Shaw interrupted. "This ain't McLennon! This here's that Joe Steelman!"

They gathered around. "Sure is!" Burwick swore viciously. "Now we're in trouble! If we don't get McLennon, we're . . ." His voice trailed away as he looked up at Dornie Shaw. The soft brown eyes were bright and boyish.

"Why, boss," he said softly, dropping his cigarette and rubbing it out with his toe, "I reckon that's where I come in. Leave McLennon to me. I'll hunt him down before sun sets tomorrow."

"Want company?" Poinsett asked.

"Don't need it," Shaw said, "but come along. I hear this Bob McLennon used to be a frontier marshal. I never liked marshals no way."

They drifted to their horses, then moved slowly away. Dornie Shaw, Poinsett, and Goff toward the west and Bob McLennon. Alton Burwick, his eyes thoughtful, rode toward the east and Mustang, and the others rode with him. Only Fessenden turned nervously and looked back. "We should have made sure they were dead."

"Ride back if you want," Clauson said. "They

are dead all right. That Kedrick! I had no use for him. I aimed my shot right for his smart skull."

Afternoon drew on. The sun lowered, and after the sun came coolness. Somewhere a coyote lifted his howl of anguish to the wide, white moon and the desert lay still and quiet beneath the sky.

In the deeper shadow of towering Chimney Rock and its bulkier neighbor, there was no movement. A coyote moved nearer, scented the blood, but with it there was the dreaded man smell. He whined anxiously and drew back, then trotted slowly off, turning only once to look back. The Appaloosa, still ground-hitched, walked along the grass toward the pool, then stopped, nostrils wide at the smell of blood. Well down behind some rocks and brush, the shooting had only made it lift its head, then return to cropping the thick, green grass that grew in the tiny, sub-irrigated area around Chimney Rock. Nothing more moved. The coolness of the night stiffened the bodies of the men who lay sprawled there.

Ten miles north Laredo Shad, late for his meeting with Kedrick, limped along the trail, leading a badly lamed horse. Two hours before, the trail along an arroyo bank had given way, and the horse had fallen. The leg was not broken, but was badly injured. Shad swore bitterly and walked on, debating as he had for the past two hours on the advisability of camping for the night. But remembering that Kedrick would be expecting him, he pushed on.

An hour later, still plodding and on blistered feet, he heard horse's hoofs and drew up, slipping his rifle into his hands. Then the rider materialized from the night, and he drew up, also. For a long minute no word was said, then Shad spoke.

"Name yourself, pardner."

The other rider also held a gun. "Bob McLennon," he said. "Who are you?"

"Laredo Shad. My horse lamed himself. I'm headed for Chimney Rock. S'posed to meet Kedrick there." He stared at the rider. "Thought you was to be at the meetin'? What happened?"

"I didn't make it. Steelman an' Slagle went. I'm ridin' up here because they never come in."

"What?" Shad's exclamation was sharp. "McLennon, I was right afeared o' that. My bet is there's been dirty work. Nevah trusted that there Burwick, not no way."

McLennon studied the Texan, liking the man, but hesitant. "What's your brand read, Laredo? You a company man?"

Shad shook his head. "Well, now, it's like this. I come in here, drawin' warrior pay to do some gun slingin', but I'm a right uppity sort of a gent about some things. This here didn't size up right to me, nor to Kedrick, so we been figurin' on gettin' shut of the company. Kedrick only stayed on, hopin' he could make peace. I stayed along with him."

"Get up behind me," McLennon said. "My horse will carry double an' it ain't far."

X

His eyes were open a long time before realization came, and he was lying in a clean, orderly place with which he was totally unfamiliar. For a long time he lay there, searching his memory for clues to tie all this together. He was Captain Tom Kedrick . . . he had gone west from New Orleans . . . he had taken on a job . . . then he remembered. There had been a meeting at Chimney Rock and Steelman had come in place of McLennon, and then he had thrown his cigarette away and had seen those men behind the rocks, seen the sunlight flashing on their rifle barrels actually. He had yelled, and then dropped, but not fast enough. He had been hit in the head, and he had been hit in the body at least once.

How long ago was that? He turned his head and found himself in a square, stone room. One side of the room was native rock, and part of another side. The rest had been built up from loose stones gathered and shaped to fit. Besides the wide bed on which he lay, there was a table and a chair.

He turned slightly, and the bed creaked. The door opened, and he looked up into the eyes of Connie Duane!

"Connie?" He was surprised. "Where is this place? What's happened?"

"You've been unconscious for days," she told him, coming to the bedside. "You have had a bad concussion and you lost a lot of blood before Laredo and Bob McLennon found you."

"What about the others?"

"Both of them are dead, and by all rights you should have been."

"But where are we? What is this place?"

"It's a cliff dwelling, a lonely one, and very ancient. It is high up in the side of the mountain called Thieving Rock. McLennon knew where it was, and he knew that, if word got out that you were alive, they would be out to complete the job at once, so they brought you here, McLennon did, with Shad."

"Are they still here?"

"Shad is. He hunts and goes to Yellow Butte for supplies, but he has to be very careful because it looked like they are beginning to get suspicious."

"McLennon?"

"He's dead, Tom. Dornie Shaw killed him. He went to Mustang to find a doctor for you, and encountered Dornie on the street. Bob was very fast, you know, but Dornie is incredible! He killed Bob before he could get a shot off."

"How did you get here?"

"Bob McLennon and Shad had talked about it, and also that Uncle John had been killed, so they came to me, and I came out here right away. I know a little about nursing, but not much. Laredo has been wonderful, Tom, he's a true friend."

Kedrick nodded. "Who did the shooting? I thought it was Poinsett."

"He was one of them. I heard them talking about it but wasn't sure until later. Poinsett was there, Goff, Fessenden, Clauson, and Shaw."

"Anything else happened?"

"Too much. They burned Yellow Butte's saloon and livery stable, and they have driven almost half the people off the land. Their surveyors are on the land now, checking the survey they made previously. A handful of the squatters have drawn back into the mountains somewhere, under Pit Laine and that friend of yours, Dai Reid. They are trying to make a stand there."

"What about Sue?"

She looked at him quickly. "You liked her, didn't you? Well, Sue has taken up with Keith. They are together all the time. He's a big man now. They've brought in some more gunmen, and the Mixus boys are still here. Right now Alton Burwick and Loren Keith have this country right under their thumbs. In fact, they even called an election."

"An election?"

"Yes, and they counted the ballots themselves. Keith was elected mayor, and Fessenden is sheriff. Burwick stayed out of it, of course, and Dornie Shaw wouldn't take the sheriff's job."

"Looks like they've got everything their own way, doesn't it?" he mused. "So they don't know I'm alive."

"No. Shad went back there and dug three graves. He buried the other two, and then filled in the third grave and put a marker over it with your name on it."

"Good!" Kedrick was satisfied. He looked up at the girl. "And how do you get out here and back without them becoming curious?"

She flushed slightly. "I haven't been back, Tom. I stayed here with you. There was no chance of going back and forth. I just left everything and came away."

"How long before I can be up?"

"Not long, if you rest. And you've talked enough now."

Kedrick turned over the whole situation in his mind. There could be no more than a few days before the sale of the land would come off, and, if there was one thing that mattered, it was that the company not be permitted to profit from their crookedness. As he lay there resting, a plan began to form in his mind, and the details supplied themselves one by one as he considered it.

His guns hung on a nail driven into the wall

183

close to his hand. His duffel, which he had brought way from the St. James, lay in the corner. It was almost dark before he completed his planning, and, when Laredo came in, he was ready for him.

"Cimarron?" Shad shook his head. "Bloomfield would be nearer. How's that?"

"Good!" Kedrick agreed. "Make it fast."

"That ain't worryin' me," Laredo said, rolling his tobacco in his jaws. "They've been mighty suspicious lately. Suppose they trail this place down while I'm gone?"

"We'll have to chance that. Here's the message. Hurry it up!"

The sun was bright in the room when Connie came through the door with his breakfast. She turned, and her face went white. "Oh, you're up!"

He grinned shakily. "That's right. I've laid abed long enough. How long has it been?"

"Almost two weeks," she told him, "but you mustn't stand up. Sit down and rest."

There was a place by a window where he had a good view of the trail below. At his request Connie brought the Winchester to him, and her own rifle. He cleaned them both, oiled them carefully, and placed them beside his window. Then he checked his guns and returned them to their holsters, digging the two Walch Navy pistols from his duffel and checking them, also.

184

Thoughtfully he considered. It was late to do anything now, but it was a wonder he had not thought of Ransome before. No more able legislator existed in Washington than Frederic Ransome, and the two had been brother officers in the Civil War as well as friends in France during the Franco-Prussian War when Ransome had been there as an observer. If anybody could block the sale to the company, he could, even on such short notice. His telegram would be followed by a letter supplying all the details, and with that to go on, Ransome might get something done. He was a popular and able young senator with good connections and an affable manner. Moreover, he was an excellent strategist. It would make all the difference in this situation.

The cliff dwelling was built well back from the face of the cliff, and evidently constructed with an eye toward concealment as well as defense. They had called this, Connie told him, Thieving Rock long before the white man appeared, and the Indians who lived here had been notorious thieves. There was a spring, so water was not a worry, and there were supplies enough for immediate purposes.

Two days dragged slowly by, and on the morning of the third Kedrick was resuming his station by the window when he saw a rider coming into the narrow cañon below. The man was moving slowly and studying the ground as he came, although from time to time he paused and searched the area with careful eyes. Kedrick pushed himself up from his chair and, taking the Winchester, worked his way along the wall to the next room.

"Connie," he called softly. There was no reply, and after a minute he called a second time. Still no answer.

Worried now, he remembered she had said something about going down below to gather some squaw cabbage to add greens to their diet.

Back at the window, he studied the terrain carefully, and then his heart gave a leap, for Connie Duane was gathering squaw cabbage from a niche in the cañon wall, not fifty yards from the unknown rider!

Lifting his rifle, Kedrick checked the range. It was all of four hundred yards and a downhill shot. Carefully he sighted on the rider. He was nearer the girl now, and a miss might ricochet and kill Connie, for the cañon wall would throw any bullet he fired back into the cañon itself and it might even ricochet several times in the close confines.

Yet, somehow, she had to be warned. If the rider saw her tracks, he would find both the girl and the hide-out. Suddenly the ears of his horse came up sharply, and the rider stiffened warily and looked all around. Carefully Kedrick drew a bead on the man again. He hated to kill an unwarned man, but if necessary he would not hesitate.

Connie was standing straight now and appeared to be listening. Tense in every fiber, Tom Kedrick watched and waited. The two were now within fifty feet of each other, although each was concealed by a corner of rock and some desert growth including a tall cottonwood and some cedars.

Still listening, both stood rigidly, and Kedrick touched his lips with the tip of his tongue. His eyes blurred with the strain, and he brushed his hand across them.

The rider was swinging to the ground now, and he had drawn a gun. Warily he stepped out from his ground-hitched horse. Shifting his eyes to Connie, Tom saw the girl wave, and, lifting his hand, he waved back, then lifted the rifle. She waved a vigorous negation with her arm, and he relaxed, waiting.

Now the man was studying tracks in the sandy bottom of the wash, and, as he knelt, his eyes riveted upon the ground, a new element entered the picture. A flicker of movement caught the tail of Kedrick's eye, and, turning his head, he saw Laredo Shad riding into the scene. He glanced swiftly at the window and waved his hand. Then he moved forward and swung to the ground.

From his vantage point Kedrick could hear nothing, but he saw Laredo approach, making heavy going of it in the thick sand, and then, not a dozen yards from the man, he stopped. He must have spoken, for the strange rider stiffened as if shot, then slowly got to his feet. As he turned, Tom saw his face fully in the sunlight. It was Clauson!

What happened then was too fast for the eye to follow. Somebody must have spoken, but who did not matter. Clauson's gun was drawn, and he started to swing it up. Laredo Shad in a gunman's crouch flashed his right-hand gun. It sprang clear, froze for a long instant, and then just as Clauson fired, Shad fired—but a split second sooner!

Clauson staggered a step back, and Shad fired again. The outlaw went down slowly, and Laredo walked forward and stripped his gun belts from him, then from his horse he took his saddlebags, rifle, and ammunition. Gathering up the dead man, and, working with Connie's help, they tied him to the saddle, and then turned the horse loose with a slap on the hip.

Connie Duane's face was white when she came into the room. "You saw that?"

He nodded. "We didn't dare to let him go. If we had, we would all have been dead before noon tomorrow. Now"—he said with grim satisfaction—"they have something to think about!"

Shad grinned at him when he came in. "I didn't see that gun he had drawed," he said ruefully. "Had it layin' along his leg as he was crouched there. Might've got me."

He dropped the saddlebags. "Mite of grub," he said, "an' some shells. I reckon we can use 'em even though we have some. The message got off, an' so did the letter. Feller over to the telegraph office was askin' a powerful lot of questions. Seems like they've been hearin' about this scrape."

"Good! The more the better. We can stand it, but the company can't. Hear anything?"

"Uh-huh. Somebody from outside the state is startin' a row about Gunter's death. I hear they have you marked for that. That is, the company is sayin' you did it."

Kedrick nodded. "They would try that. Well, in a couple of days I'll be out of here and then we'll see what can be done."

"You take some time," Shad said dubiously. "That passel o' thieves ain't goin' to find us. Although," he said suddenly, "I saw the tracks of that grulla day afore yestiddy, an' not far off."

The grulla again!

XI

Two more days drifted by, and Tom Kedrick ventured down the trail and the ladders to the cañon below with Laredo and visited their horses concealed in a tiny glade not far away. The Appaloosa nickered and trotted toward him, and

Kedrick grinned and scratched his chest. "How's it, boy? Ready to go places?"

"He's askin' for it," Shad said. He lighted a smoke and squinted his eyes at Kedrick. "What do you aim to do when you do move?"

"Ride around a little. I aim to see Pit Laine, an' then I'm goin' to start hunting up every mother's son that was in that dry-gulching. Especially," he added, "Dornie Shaw."

"He's bad," Laredo said quietly. "I nevah seen it, but you ask Connie. Shaw's chain lightnin'. She seen him kill Bob."

"So one of us dies," Kedrick said quietly. "I'd go willing enough to take him with me, an' a few others."

"That's it. He's a killer, but the old bull o' that woods is Alton Burwick, believe me, he is. Keith is just right-hand man for him, an' the fall guy if they need one. Burwick's the poison-mean one."

With Connie they made their start three days later, and rode back trails beyond the rim to the hide-out Laine had established. It was Dai Reid himself who stopped them, and his eyes lighted up when he saw Kedrick.

"Ah, Tom!" His broad face beamed. "Like my own son, you are. We'd heard you were kilt dead."

Pit Laine was standing by the fire, and around him on the ground were a dozen men, most of whom Kedrick recognized. They sat up slowly as the three walked into the open space, and Pit turned. It was the first time Kedrick had seen him, and he was surprised. He was scarcely taller than his sister, but wide in the shoulders and slim in the hips. When he turned, he faced them squarely, and his eyes were sharp and bitter. This was a killing man, Kedrick decided, as dangerous in his own way as that pocket-size devil, Dornie Shaw.

"I'm Kedrick," he said, "and this is Connie Duane. I believe you know Shad."

"We know all of you." Laine watched them, his eyes alert and curious.

Quietly and concisely, Kedrick explained, and ended by saying: "So there it is. I've asked this friend of mine to start an investigation into the whole mess, and to block the sale until the truth is clear. Once the sale is blocked and that investigation started, they won't be with us long. They could get away with this only if they could keep it covered up, and they had a fair chance of doing that."

"So we wait and let them run off?" Laine demanded.

"No." Tom Kedrick shook his head decidedly. "We ride into Mustang . . . all of us. They have the mayor and the sheriff, but public opinion is largely on our side. Furthermore," he said quietly, "we ride in the minute they get the news the sale is blocked. Once that news is around town, they will have no friends. The band wagon riders will get off, and fast."

"There'll be shootin'," one old-timer opined.

"Some," Kedrick admitted, "but, if I have my way, there'll be more of hanging. There's killers in that town, the bunch that dry-gulched Steelman and Slagle. The man who killed Bob McLennon is the man I want."

Pit Laine turned. "I want him."

"Sorry, Laine. He killed Bob, an' Bob was only in town to get a doc for me. You may," he added, "get your chance, anyway."

"I'd like a shot at him my ownself," Laredo said quietly, "but somethin' else bothers me. Who's this grulla rider? Is he one of you?"

"Gets around plenty," the old-timer said, "but nobody ever sees him. I reckon he knows this here country better'n any of us. He must've been aroun' here for a long time."

"What's he want?" Shad wondered aloud. "That don't figure."

Kedrick shrugged. "I'd like to know." He turned to Dai. "It's good to see you. I was afraid you'd had trouble."

"Trouble?" Dai smiled his wide smile. "It's trouble, you say? All my life there's been trouble, and where man is, there will be trouble to the end of time, if not of one kind, then another. But I take my trouble as it comes." He drew deeply on his short-stemmed pipe and glanced at the scar around Kedrick's skull. "Looks like you'd a bit of it yourself. If you'd a less hard skull, you'd now be dead."

"I'd not have given a plugged *peso* for him when I saw him," Laredo said dryly. "The three of them lyin' there, bloody an' shot up. We thought for sure they was all dead. This one, he'd a hole through him, low down an' mean, an' that head of his looked like it had been smashed until we moved him. He was lucky as well as thick-skulled."

Morning found Laredo and Kedrick once more in the saddle. Connie Duane had stayed behind with some of the squatters' women. Together the two men were pushing on toward Mustang, but taking their time, for they had no desire to be seen or approached by any of the company riders.

"There's nothing much we can do," Kedrick agreed, "but I want to know the lay of the land in town. It's mighty important to be able to figure out what will happen when the news hits the place. Right now, everything is right for them. Alton Burwick and Loren Keith are better off than they ever were. Just size it up. They came in here with the land partly held by squatters, with a good claim on the land. That land they managed to get surveyed and they put in their claim to the best of it, posted the notices, and waited them out.

If somebody hadn't seen one of those notices and read it, the whole sale might have gone through and nobody the wiser. Somebody did see it, and trouble started. They had two mighty able men to contend with, Slagle and McLennon. Well, both of them are dead now. And Steelman, another possible leader, is dead, too. So far as they are aware, nobody knows anything about the deaths of those men or who caused them. I was the one man they had learned they couldn't depend on, and they think I'm dead. John Gunter brought money into the deal, and he's dead and out of the picture completely. A few days more and the sale goes through, the land becomes theirs, and there isn't any organized opposition now. Pit Laine and his group will be named as outlaws, and hunted as such, and, believe me, once the land sale goes through, Keith will be hunting them with a posse of killers."

"Yeah," Laredo drawled, "they sure got it sewed up, looks like. But you're forgettin' one thing. You're forgettin' the girl, Connie Duane."

"What about her?"

"Look," Shad said, speaking around his cigarette, "she sloped out of town, right after McLennon was killed. They thought she had been talking to you before, and she told 'em off in the office, said she was gettin' her money out of it. All right, so suppose she asks for it, and they can't pay? Suppose," he added, "she begins to talk

194

and tells what she knows, and they must figure it's plenty. She was Gunter's niece, and for all they knew he told her more than he did tell her."

"You mean they'll try to get hold of her?"

"What do you think? They'll try to get hold of her, or kill her."

Tom Kedrick's eyes narrowed. "She'll be safe with Laine," he said, but an element of doubt was in his voice. "That's a good crowd."

Shad shrugged. "Maybe. Don't forget that Singer was one of them, but he didn't hesitate to try to kill Sloan, or to point him out for Abe Mixus. He was bought off by the company, so maybe there are others."

At that very moment, in the office of the gray stone building, such a man sat opposite Alton Burwick, while Keith sat in a chair against the wall. The man's name was Hirst. His face was sallow, but determined. "I ain't lyin'," he said flatly. "I rode all night to git here, slippin' out o' camp on the quiet. She rode in with that gunman, Laredo Shad, and this Kedrick *hombre*."

"Kedrick! Alive?" Keith sat forward, his face tense.

"Alive as you or me! Had him most of the hair clipped on one side of his head, an' a bad scab there. He sort of favored his side, too. Oh, he'd been shot all right, but he's ridin' now, believe me!"

The renegade had saved the worst until last. He smiled grimly at Burwick. "I can use some money, Mister Burwick," he said, "an' there's more I could tell you."

Burwick stared at him, his eyes glassy hard, then reached into a drawer and threw two gold eagles on the desk. "All right! What can you tell me?"

"Kedrick sent a message to some *hombre* in Washington name of Ransome. He's to block the sale of the land until there's a complete investigation."

"What?"

Keith came to his feet, his face ashen. This was beyond his calculations. When the idea had first been brought to his attention, it had seemed a very simple, easy way to turn a fast profit. He had excellent connections in Washington through his military career, and with Burwick managing things on the other end and Gunter with the money, it seemed impossible to beat it. He was sure to net a handsome profit, clear his business with Gunter and Burwick, then return East and live quietly on the profits. That it was a crooked deal did not disturb him, but that his friends in the East might learn of it!

"Ransome!" His voice was shocked. "Of all people!"

Frederic Ransome had served with him in the war, and their mutual relationship had been something less than friendly. There had been that episode by the bridge. He flushed at the thought of it, but Ransome knew, and Ransome would use it as a basis for judgment. Kedrick had no way of knowing just how fortunate his choice of Ransome had been.

"That does it!" He got to his feet. "Ransome will bust this wide open, and love it!"

He was frightened, and Burwick could see it. He sat there, his gross body filling the chair, wearing the same soiled shirt. His eyes followed Keith with irritation and contempt. Was Keith going bad on him now?

"Get back there," Burwick said to Hirst, "and keep me informed of all movements. Watch everything closely now, and don't miss a trick. You will be paid."

When Hirst had gone, Burwick turned to Keith and smiled with his fat lips. "So does it matter if they slow it up a little? Let them have their investigation. It will come too late."

"Too late?" Keith was incredulous. "With such witnesses against us as Kedrick, Shad, Connie, and the rest of them?"

"When the time comes," Burwick said quietly, "there will be no witnesses. Believe me, there won't be!"

XII

Keith turned on Burwick, puzzled by the sound of his voice. "What do you mean?" he asked.

Burwick chuckled and rolled his fat lips on his cigar. There was malice and some contempt in the look he gave Keith. How much better, he thought, had Kedrick not been so namby-pamby. He was twice the man Keith was, for all the latter's commanding presence.

"Why," he said, "if there's no witnesses, there'll be no case. What can these people in town tell them? What they suspect? Suspicions won't stand in a court of law, nor with that committee. By the time they get here, this country will be peaceful and quiet, believe me."

"What do you want to do?" Keith demanded.

"Do? What is there to do? Get rid of Kedrick, Laredo Shad, and that girl. Then you'll take a posse and clean out that rat's nest back of the rim. Then who will they talk to? Gunter might have weakened, but he's dead. With the rest of them out of it . . ."

"Not Connie," Keith protested. "Not her! For heaven's sake, man!"

Burwick snorted and his lips twisted in an angry sneer as he heaved his bulk from the chair. "Yes, Connie!" he said. "Are you a complete

198

fool, Keith? Or have you gone soft? That girl knows more than all of them. Suppose Gunter talked to her, and he most likely did? She'll know everything, everything, I tell you!"

He paced back across the room, measuring Keith. The fool! He was irritated and angry. The sort of men they made these days, a weak and sniveling crowd. Keith had played out his time. If he finished this job alive . . . well, Dornie didn't like Keith. Burwick chuckled suddenly. Dornie! Now there was a man! The way he had killed that Bob McLennon!

"Now get this. Get the boys together. Get Fessenden, Goff, Clauson, Poinsett, and the Mixus boys and send them out with Dornie. I want those three killed, you hear me? I want them dead before the week is out, and no bodies, understand?"

Keith touched his dry lips, his eyes haunted. He had bargained for nothing like this. It had all seemed such an easy profit, and only a few poverty-stricken squatters to prevent them from acquiring wealth in a matter of a few months. Everything had started off just as Burwick had suggested, everything had gone so well. Gunter had provided the money, and he had fronted for them in Washington. Uneasily now Keith realized that, if trouble was made over this, it would be he upon whom the blame would rest. Burwick somehow had been in the background in the East as much as he, Keith, had been kept in the background here. Yet it would be his guilt if anything went wrong. And with Ransome investigating, everything had gone wrong.

He sighed deeply. Of course, Burwick was right. There was only one thing to do now. At least, Dornie and the others would not hesitate. Suddenly he remembered something.

"You mentioned Clauson. He's out of it, Burwick. Clauson came in last night tied to his horse. He had been dead for hours."

"What?" Burwick stopped his pacing and walked up to Keith. "You just remembered?" He held his face inches away from Keith's and glared. "Is anybody backtracking that horse? You blithering idiot! Clauson was dynamite with a gun, so if he's dead, shot, it has to be by one of three men, and you know it!"

Burwick's face was dark with passion and he wheeled and walked the length of the room, swearing in a low, violent voice that shocked Keith with its deep, underlying passion. When he turned again, Burwick's eyes were ugly with fury. "Can't you realize," he demanded hoarsely, "those men are dangerous? That every second they are alive we are in danger? You have seen Dornie in action. Well, believe me, I'd sooner have him after me than Kedrick. I know Kedrick! He's a former Army officer . . . that's what you're thinking all the time . . . an officer and a gentleman. But he's something more, do you hear? He's more. He's a gentleman . . . that's true enough . . . but the man's a fighter, he loves to fight! Under all the calmness and restraint there's a drive and power that Dornie Shaw could never equal. Dornie may be faster, and I think he is, but don't you forget for one instant that Kedrick won't be through until he's down, down and dead."

Loren Keith was shocked. In his year's association with Burwick he had never seen the man in a passion, and had never heard him speak with such obvious respect, and even—yes, even fear—of any man. What had Alton Burwick seen that he himself had not seen?

He stared at Burwick, puzzled and annoyed, but some of the man's feeling began to transmit itself to him, and he became distinctly uneasy. He bit his lips and watched Burwick pacing angrily.

"It's not only him, but it's Shad. That cool, thin-faced Texan. As for Laine . . ."—Burwick's eyes darkened—"he may be the worst of the lot. He thinks he has a personal stake in this."

"Personal?" Keith looked inquiringly at the older man. "What do you mean?"

Burwick dismissed the question with a gesture. "No matter. They must go, all of them, and right now." He turned and his eyes were cold. "Keith, you fronted us in Washington. If this thing goes wrong, you're the one who will pay. Now go out there and get busy. You've a little time, and you've the men. Get busy!"

When he had gone, Burwick dropped into his chair and stared blindly before him. It had gone too far to draw back even if he was so inclined, and he was not. The pity of it was that there had been no better men to be had than Keith and Gunter. Yet, everything could still go all right, for he would know how to meet any investigating committee, how to soft-pedal the trouble, turn it off into a mere cow-country quarrel of no moment and much exaggerated. The absence of any complaining witness would leave them helpless to proceed, and he could make it seem a mere teapot tempest. Keith was obviously afraid of Ransome. Well, he was not.

Burwick was still sitting there when the little cavalcade of horsemen streamed by, riding out of town on their blood trail. The number had been augmented, he noticed, by four new arrivals, all hard, desperate men. Even without Keith, they might do the job. He heaved himself to his feet and paced across the room, staring out the window. It went badly with him to see Connie Duane die, for he had plans for Connie—maybe. His eyes narrowed.

Out on the desert the wind stirred restlessly, and in the brassy sky above a lone buzzard circled as if aware of the creeping tension that was slowly gripping the country beneath it. Far to the north, toward Durango, a cattle buyer pulled his team to a halt and studied the sky. There was no hint of storm, yet he had felt uneasy ever since leaving town on his buying trip down to Yellow Butte and Mustang. There had been rumors of trouble down that way, but then there had been intermittent trouble there for some time, and he was not alarmed. Yet he was somehow uneasy, as though the very air carried a warning.

South of him, and below the rim, Laredo Shad and Kedrick turned aside from the Mustang trail and headed toward Yellow Butte. It was only a little way out of their line of travel, but both men wanted to see what had happened there. Yet, when they approached the town, aside from the blackened ruins of the destroyed buildings, everything seemed peaceful and still. Eight or ten families had moved back into the town and a few had never left. They looked up warily as the two riders drew near, then nodded a greeting.

They knew now that these two were siding with them against the company, but hardship and struggle had wearied them, and they watched the two enter the settlement without excitement. The saloon had opened its doors in the large roomy office of the livery stable, and they went there now. A couple of men leaned on the bar, and both turned as they entered, greeted them, and returned to their conversation.

It was growing cool outside and the warmth of the room felt good. Both men stepped to the bar, and Kedrick ordered and paid. Shad toyed with his drink. He seemed uneasy, and finally he turned to Tom. "I don't like it," he said, low-voiced, "somehow or other Burwick is goin' to know about Ransome, an' he'll be in a sweat to get Connie out of the way, an' you an' me with her."

Kedrick agreed, for his own mind had been reading sign along the same trail. The only way out for the company now was to face the committee, if Ransome managed one, with a plausible tale and an accomplished fact, and then let them make the most of it.

"Burwick's a snake," Shad commented. "He'll never quit wigglin' until the sun goes down for the last time. Not that one. He's in this deep, an' he ain't the man to lose without a fight."

Horses' hoofs sounded on the road outside, and, when they turned, Pit Laine and Dai Reid were dismounting before the door. They walked in, and Laine looked at Kedrick, then moved on to the bar. Dai looked worried, but said nothing. After a minute, Laine turned suddenly and went outside. "What's the matter?" Kedrick asked.

"It be worry, and some of it shame, an' all for that sister o' his. Who would think it o' her? To go over to the other side? He's that shy about it, you would scarce believe. When a man looks at him, he thinks it's his sister they are thinkin' on, and how she sold out to that traitor to mankind, that rascal, Keith."

Kedrick shrugged. "Ambition and money do strange things. She has the makings of a woman, too."

Laine opened the door. "Better come out," he said, "we've got trouble."

They crowded outside. Men were hurrying toward the houses, their faces grave. "What is it?" Kedrick asked quickly.

"Burt Williams signaled from the top of the butte. There's riders coming from Mustang, a bunch of them."

As they looked, the small dark figure of a man appeared on the edge of the mesa once more. This time they saw his arm wave, once—two—three times, and continue until he had waved it six times. When he had completed, he gestured to the southeast. Then he signaled four more times from the southwest.

"Ten riders," Laine spat. "Well, we've got more than that here, but they aren't as salty as that crowd."

Burt Williams, favoring his broken arm, knelt behind a clump of brush on top of Yellow Butte and studied the approaching horsemen through the glass. He knew all in this group by sight but not by favor. One by one he named them off to himself: "Keith, Dornie Shaw, Fessenden, an'

Goff . . . Poinsett. No, that's not Poinsett. That's one of the Mixus boys. Yep, an' there's the other."

He swung his glass. The four riders, spaced well apart, were approaching at a steady pace. None of their faces was familiar. He stared at them a while, but finally placed only one of them, a badman from Durango who ran with Port Stockton and the Ketchum outfit. His name was Brokow.

Stirred, he searched the country all around the town for other movement, then turned back to the larger cavalcade of riders. Had he held on a certain high flat a minute longer he would have seen two unmounted men cross it at a stooping run and drop into the wide arroyo northeast of town. As it was, he had been studying the approaching group for several minutes before he realized that Poinsett was not among them. He was with neither group.

Worried, Williams squinted his eyes against the sun, wondering how he could apprise them of the danger down below, for the absence of Poinsett disturbed him. The man was without doubt one of the most vicious of the company killers, a bitter man, made malignant by some dark happening in his past, but filled now with a special sort of venom all his own. Williams would have worried even more had he seen Poinsett at that moment.

The attack had been planned carefully and with all of Keith's skill. He surmised who they would be looking for, and hoped their watcher would overlook the absence of Poinsett, for it was he who Keith wanted in the right position, for Poinsett was unquestionably the best of the lot with a rifle. At that moment, not two hundred yards from town, Poinsett and his companion, Alf Starrett, were hunkered down in a cluster of brush and boulders at one side of the arroyo. Poinsett had his Spencer .56 and was settling into position for his first shot. Starrett, with a fifteen-shot Henry .44, was a half dozen yards away.

Poinsett pulled out a huge silver watch and consulted it. "At half after two, he says. All right, that's when he'll get it." With utmost composure he began to roll a smoke, and Alf Starrett, a hard-faced and wizened little man, noticed that his fingers were steady as he sifted tobacco into the paper.

Bob McLennon had planned the defense of Yellow Butte, if such a defense became neces-sary, and, while Bob had been something of a hand with a gun, he definitely had not been a soldier or even an Indian fighter. Moreover, they had not expected an all-out battle for the town. Whatever the reason, he had committed a fatal error, for that pile of boulders and brush offered almost perfect concealment while affording com-plete coverage of the town, its one street, and the back as well as front of most of the buildings.

Keith had been quick to see this on his earlier

visits to the town, and had planned to have Poinsett and Starrett approach the place some time before the main force moved in. In this, owing to their own experience, they had been successful.

Poinsett finished his cigarette and took up his rifle, then settled down to careful watching and checking of the time. He had his orders and they were explicit. He was to fire on the first target offered after half past two—and his first shot must kill.

Shad and Kedrick had returned to the saloon and Pit Laine was loitering in front. Dai had gone across the street. Laine was in a position out of sight of Poinsett, but the latter had glimpsed Dai. The Welshman, however, offered only a fleeting target and Poinsett did not consider firing. His chance came at once, however.

The door of one of the nearest shacks opened and a man came out. He wore a broad-brimmed gray hat, torn at the crown, and a large-checked shirt tucked into jeans supported by suspenders. He turned at the door and kissed his wife. Poinsett took careful aim with his .56, choosing as his target point the man's left suspender buckle. Taking a good, deep breath, he held it and squeezed off his shot.

The big bullet struck with a heavy thump. The man took a lurch sidewise, tried to straighten, then went down. His wife ran from the door, screaming. Up the street a door banged and two men ran into the street, staring. Starrett's first shot knocked the rifle from the hand of one, splintering the stock. Poinsett dropped his man, but the fellow began to drag himself, favoring one leg that even at this distance they could see covered with a dark blotch at the knee.

Poinsett was a man without mercy. Coolly and carefully he squeezed off his second shot. The man stiffened, jerked spasmodically, and lay still.

"Missed my man," Alf said, apologetically, "but I ruint his shootin' iron."

Poinsett spat, his eyes cold. "Could happen to anybody," he said philosophically, "but I figured you burnt him anyways."

Within the saloon Kedrick had a glass half to his mouth when the shot boomed, followed almost at once by two more, their reports sounding almost as one.

"Blazes!" Shad whirled. "They ain't here yet?"

"They've been here," Kedrick said with quick realization. He swung to the door, glancing up the street. He saw the body of the last man to fall and, leaning out a bit, glimpsed the other. His lips tightened, for neither man was moving.

"Somebody is up the draw," he explained quickly. "He's got the street covered. Is there a back door?"

Kedrick dove for the door followed by the others once the bartender indicated the way, then caught up his shotgun. His pockets were already stuffed with shells. At the door Kedrick halted, then, flattened against the wall, stared up the draw. From here he could see the edge of the bunch of boulders and guessed the fire came from there. "Pinned down," he said. "They are up the draw."

Nobody moved. His memory for terrain served him to good purpose now. Recalling the draw, he remembered that it was below the level of the town beyond that point, but right there the boulders offered a perfect firing point.

Scattered shots came from down the draw, and nobody spoke. All knew that the three men down there could not long withstand the attack and would fall back on the town to be taken in the rear.

XIII

Kedrick made up his mind quickly. Defense of the town was now impossible and they would be wiped out or burned alive if they attempted to remain here. "Shad," he said quickly, "get across the street to Dai and Pit. Yell out to the others and get them to fall back, regardless of risk, to the cañon at the foot of Yellow Butte."

He took a step back and glanced at the trap

door to the roof. The bartender saw the intent and shook his head. "You can't do it, boy. They'd git you from down the crick."

"I'm going to chance it. I think they are still too far off. If I can give you folks covering fire, you may make it."

"What about you?" Shad demanded.

"I'll make it. Get moving!"

Laredo wheeled and darted to the door, paused an instant, and lunged across the street. The bartender hesitated, swore softly, then followed. Kedrick picked up a bottle of the liquor and shoved it into his shirt, then jumped for the edge of the trap door, caught it, and pulled himself through into the small attic. Carefully he studied the situation.

Hot firing came from downstream, and evidently the killers were momentarily stopped there. He hoisted himself through, swung to the ridge of the roof, and carefully studied the boulders. Suddenly he caught a movement, and knew that what he had first believed to be a gray rock was actually a shirt. He took careful aim with his Winchester, then fired.

The gray shirt jumped, and a hand flew up, then fell loose. Instantly a Spencer boomed and a bullet tore a chunk from the ridgepole near his face and splattered him with splinters. Kedrick moved downroof a bit, then, catching the signal from the window across the street, he deliberately shoved his rifle and head up and fired four fast shots, then two more.

Ducking his head, he reloaded the Winchester. Another bullet smashed the ridgepole and then a searching fire began, the heavy slugs tearing through the roof about three to four inches below the top.

Kedrick slid down the roof, hesitated at the edge of the trap door, and, seeing a distant figure circling to get behind the men in the wash, he took careful aim and squeezed off his shot. It was all of five hundred yards, and he had only a small bit of darkness at which to aim.

The shot kicked up sand short of the mark by a foot or more as nearly as he could judge, and he knew he had missed, but the would-be sniper lost his taste for his circling movement and slid out of sight. Kedrick went down the trap door and dropped again into the livery stable office. Regretfully he glanced at the stock of whiskey, then picked up two more bottles and stuffed them into his pockets.

Hesitating only a second, he lunged across the way for the shelter of the livery stable. The Spencer boomed and he knew that the hidden marksmen had been awaiting this effort. He felt the shock of the bullet, staggered, but kept going.

Reaching the livery stable, he felt the coldness of something on his stomach and glanced down. The bottle in his shirt had been broken by the bullet and he smelled to high heaven of good whiskey. Picking the glass out of his shirt, he located his horse's stall, led the Appaloosa out into the runway, and swung into the saddle.

The Spencer boomed again and again as he hit the road, riding hard, but he made it. The others cheered as he rode pell-mell through the cañon mouth and swung to the ground.

"This is no good," Laine said. "They can get behind us on the ridge."

Two men limped in from the draw, having withdrawn from boulder to boulder. Kedrick glanced around. There were fourteen men and women here who were on their feet. One man, he who had had the rifle knocked from his hand, had a shattered arm. The others were slightly wounded. Of them all, he had only seven men able to fight.

Quickly he gave directions for their retreat, then with Dai and Shad to hold the cañon mouth and cover them, they started back up the cañon.

Tom Kedrick measured his group thoughtfully. Of Laredo, Dai, and Laine, he had no doubts at all. Of these others, he could not be sure. Good men, some of them, and one or two were obviously frightened. Nobody complained, however, and one of the men whose face was pale took a wounded man's rifle and gave him a shoulder on which to lean. He led them to the crevasse, and down into it.

Amazed, they stared around. "What d'you know?" the bartender spat. "Been here nigh seven year an' never knowed o' this place!"

There were four horses with the group, and they brought them all into the cave. One of the men complained, but Kedrick turned on him. "There's water, but we may be glad to eat horse meat." The man swallowed and stared.

Laine pointed at Kedrick's shirt. "Man, you're bleedin'!"

Kedrick grinned. "That isn't blood, it's whiskey! They busted one of the bottles I brought away!"

Pit chuckled. "I'd 'most as soon it was blood," he said, "seems a waste of good likker."

The seven able men gathered near the escape end of the crevasse, and one of them grinned at Kedrick. "I wondered how you got away so slick. Is there another way out down here?"

He shook his head. "If there is, I don't know it. I waited and got out through the cañon when it wasn't watched."

Laine's face was serious. "They could hold us here," he said anxiously. "We'd be stuck for sure."

Kedrick nodded. "I'm taking an extra canteen and some grub, then I'm going atop the butte to join Burt Williams. I'd like one man with me. From up there we can hold them off, I think."

"I'm your man," Laredo said quietly. "Wait'll I get my gear."

A rifle boomed, and then Dai Reid joined them. "They are comin' up," he said. He glanced at Kedrick. "One man is dead in the boulders. I got the look of him by my glass. It was Alf Starrett. Poinsett was the other."

"Starrett was a skunk," Burnett, one of the settlers, said, "a low-down skunk. He kilt a man up Kansas way, an' a man disappeared from his outfit oncet that occasioned considerable doubt if he didn't git hisself another."

Kedrick turned to Pit Laine. "Looks like your show down here," he said. "Don't open fire until you have to, and don't fire even one shot unless it's needed. We'll be on top."

He led the way out of the crevasse and into the boulders and brush behind it. There was no sign of the attackers, and he surmised they were holed up, awaiting the arrival of some supporting fire from the rim back of the cañon.

Tom glanced up at the towering butte. It reared itself all of a hundred and fifty feet above him and most of it totally without cover. As they waited, a rifle boomed high above them and there was a puff of dust in the cañon mouth. Burt Williams had opened up, in spite of his wounded arm.

Yet their first move toward the butte drew fire, and Laredo drew back. "No chance. We'll have to wait until dark. You reckon they'll hit us before then?"

"If they do, they won't get far." Tom Kedrick

215

hunkered well down among the slabs of rock at the foot of the Butte. "We've got us a good firing point right here." He rolled a smoke and lit up. "What are you planning when this is over, Shad? Do you plan to stay here?"

The tall Texan shrugged. "Ain't pondered it much. Reckon that will take care of itself. What you aimin' to do?"

"You know the Mogollons southwest of here? I figured I'd go down there and lay out a ranch for myself." He smoked thoughtfully. "Down in east Texas, before I came west, a fellow arrived there named Ikard. Had some white-faced cattle with him, and you should see 'em! Why, they have more beef on one sorry critter than three longhorns. I figured a man could get himself a few Hereford bulls and start a herd. Might even buy fifty or sixty head for a beginning, and let 'em mix with the longhorns if they like."

"I might go for somethin' like that," Laredo said quietly. "I always wanted to own a ranch. Fact is, I started one once, but had to git shut of it." He studied the end of his cigarette. "That was in the Texas Panhandle, a ways south of Tascosa. Quite a distance. It was rough country. I mean rough to live in, not rough like this is. Why, you could stand on your front step down thataway an' see straight ahead for three days! Coyotes? Why, you should see 'em! They'd whup a grizzly, or near it, an' make these coyotes around here look like jack rabbits." He stared down the cañon toward the mouth, his rifle across his knees. He did not look at Kedrick, but he commented casually: "We need luck, Cap'n, plenty of luck."

"Uh-huh"—Kedrick's face was sober—"right now we're bottled up, and, believe me, Burwick will stop at nothing. I wonder who was on watch up the cañon? Or supposed to be?"

"Somebody said his name was Hirst. Sallow-faced *hombre*."

"We'll have to talk to him. Was he down below?"

"Come to think of it, he wasn't. He must have hid out back there."

"Or sold out. Remember Singer? He wouldn't have been the only one."

Laredo rubbed out the last of his cigarette. "They'll be makin' their play soon. You know, Kedrick, I'd as soon make a break for it, get a couple of horses, an' head for Mustang. When we go, we might as well take Keith an' that dirty Burwick with us."

Kedrick nodded in agreement, but he wasn't thinking of the men below. There were at least four good men aside from Shad, Laine, and Dai Reid. That left the numbers not too unevenly balanced. The fighting skill and numbers were slightly on the enemy's side, as they had at least twelve men when the battle opened, and they had lost Starrett. That made the odds eleven to eight unless they had moved up extra men, which was highly probable. Still, they were expecting defense, not an attack.

He studied the situation. Suddenly a dark figure loomed on the rim of the cañon some hundred and fifty yards off, and much higher. He lifted his rifle and fired even as both Shad and Kedrick threw down on him with rifles, firing instantly. The man vanished, but whether hit or not they could not tell.

Desultory firing began, and from time to time they caught glimpses of men advancing from the cañon mouth, but never in sight long enough to offer a target, and usually rising from the ground some distance from where they dropped. The afternoon was drawing on, however, and the sun was setting almost in the faces of the attackers, which made their aim uncertain and their movements hesitant. Several times Shad or Kedrick dusted the oncoming party, but got in no good shots. Twice a rifle boomed from the top of the butte, and once they heard a man cry out as though hit.

"You know, Laredo," Kedrick said suddenly, "it goes against the grain to back up for those coyotes. I'm taking this grub up to Burt, an', when I come back, we're going to move down that cañon and see how much stomach they've got for a good scrap."

Shad grinned, his eyes flickering with humor.

"That's ace high with me, pardner," he said dryly. "I never was no hand for a hole, and the women are safe."

"All but one," Kedrick said, "that Missus Taggart who lives in that first house. Her husband got killed and she wouldn't leave."

"Yeah, heard one o' the womenfolk speak on it. That Taggart never had a chance. Good folks, those two."

Colonel Loren Keith stared gloomily at the towering mass of Yellow Butte. That man atop the butte had them pinned down. Now if they could just get up there. He thought of the men he had commanded in years past, and compared them with these outlaws. A pack of murderers. How had he got into this, anyway? Why couldn't a man know when he took a turning where it would lead him? It seemed so simple in the beginning to run off a bunch of one-gallused farmers and squatters.

Wealth—he had always wanted wealth, the money to pay his way in the circles where he wanted to travel, but somehow it had always eluded him, and this had seemed a wonderful chance. Bitterly he stared at the butte, and remembered the greasy edge of Burwick's shirt collar, and the malice in his eyes, Burwick who used men as he saw fit, and disposed of them when he was through.

In the beginning it hadn't seemed that way. His own commanding presence, his soldier's stride, his cold clarity of thought, all these left him despising Gunter as a mere businessman and Burwick as a conniving weakling. But then suddenly Burwick began to show his true self, and all ideas of controlling the whole show left Keith while he stared in shocked horror as the man unmasked. Alton Burwick was no dirty weakling, no mere ugly fat man, but a monster of evil, a man with a brain like a steel trap, stopping at nothing, and by his very depth of wickedness startling Keith into obedience.

Gunter had wanted to pull out. Only now would Keith admit even to himself the cause of Gunter's death, and he knew he would die as quickly. How many times had he not seen the malevolence in the eyes of Dornie Shaw, and well he knew how close Shaw stood to Burwick. In a sense, they were two of a kind.

His feeling of helplessness shocked and horrified Keith. He had always imagined himself a strong man, and had gone his way, domineering and supercilious. Now he saw himself as only a tool in the hands of a man he despised, yet unable to escape. Deep within him there was the hope that they still would pull their chestnuts out from the fire and take the enormous profit the deal promised.

One man stood large in his mind, one man drew

all his anger, his hate and bitterness. That man was Tom Kedrick. From that first day Kedrick had made him seem a fool. Keith had endeavored to put Kedrick firmly in his place, speaking of his rank and his twelve years of service, and then Kedrick had calmly paraded such an array of military experience that few men could equal, and right before them all. He had not doubted Kedrick, for vaguely now he remembered some of the stories he had heard of the man. That the stories were true, and that Kedrick was a friend of Ransome's, infuriated him still more.

He stepped into the makeshift saloon and poured a drink, staring at it gloomily. Fessenden came in, Goff with him.

"We goin' to roust them out o' there, Colonel?" Goff asked. "It will be dark soon."

Keith tossed off his drink. "Yes, right away. Are the rest of them out there?"

"All but Poinsett. He'll be along."

Keith poured another stiff shot and tossed it off as quickly, then followed them into the street of Yellow Butte.

They were all gathered there but the Mixus boys who had followed along toward the cañon, and a couple of the newcomers who had circled to get on the cliff above and beyond the boulders and brush where the squatters had taken refuge. Poinsett was walking down the road in long strides. He was abreast of the first house when a woman stepped from the door. She was a square-built woman in a faded, blue cotton dress and man's shoes, run down at the heel. She held a double-barreled shotgun in her hands, and, as Poinsett drew abreast of her, she turned on him and fired both barrels, at point-blank range, and Poinsett took them right through the middle. Almost torn in two, he hit the ground, gasping once, his blood staining the gray gravel before their shocked eyes.

The woman turned on them, and they saw that she was no longer young. Her square face was red and a few strands of graying hair blew about her face. As she looked at them, her work-roughened hands still clutching the empty shotgun, she motioned at the fallen man in the faded, checked shirt.

In that moment the fact that she was fat, growing old, and that her thick legs ended in the grotesque shoes seemed to vanish, and in the blue eyes were no tears, only her chin trembling a little as she said: "He was my man. Taggart never give me much, an' he never had it to give, but in his own way he loved me. You killed him . . . all of you. I wish I had more shells."

She turned her back on them and, without another glance, went into the house and closed the door behind her.

They stood in a grim half circle then, each man

faced suddenly with the enormity of what they were doing and had done.

Lee Goff was the first to speak. He stood spraddle-legged, his thick, hard body bulging all his clothes, his blond hair bristling. "Anybody bothers that woman," he said, "I'll kill him."

XIV

Keith led his attack just before dusk and lost two men before they withdrew, but not before they learned of the hole. Dornie Shaw squatted behind the abutment formed by the end wall of the cañon where it opened on the plain near the arroyo. "That makes it easy," he said, "we still got dynamite."

Keith's head came up, and he saw Shaw staring at him, his eyes queerly alight.

"Or does that go against the grain, Colonel? About ten sticks of dynamite dropped into that crevasse an' Burwick will get what he wants . . . no bodies."

"If there's a cave back there," Keith objected, "they'd be buried alive!"

Nobody replied. Keith's eyes wandered around to the other men, but their eyes were on the ground; they were shunning responsibility for this, and only Shaw enjoyed it. Keith shuddered. What a fool he had been to get mixed up in this!

A horse's hoof struck stone, and as one man they looked up. Saddle leather creaked, although they could not see the horse. A spur jingled, and Alton Burwick stood among them.

Loren Keith straightened to his feet and briefly explained the situation. Burwick nodded from time to time, then added: "Use the dynamite. First thing in the morning. That should end it, once and for all." He drew a cigar from his pocket and bit off the end. "Had a wire. That committee is comin' out, all right. Take them a couple of weeks to get here, an' by that time folks should be over this an' talkin' about somethin' else. I'm figurin' a bonus for you all."

He turned back toward his horse, then stopped and, catching Dornie Shaw's eye, jerked his head.

Shaw got up from the fire and followed him, and Keith stared after them, his eyes bitter. Now what? Was he being left out of something else?

Beyond the edge of the firelight and beyond the reach of their ears, Burwick paused and let Shaw come up to him. "Nice work, Dornie," he said, "we make a pair, you an' me."

"Yeah." Dornie nodded. "An' sometimes I think a pair's enough."

"Well"—Burwick puffed on his cigar—"I need a good man to side me, an' Gunter's gone . . . at least."

"That company o' yours"—Dornie was almost whispering—"had too many partners, anyway."

"Uh-huh," Burwick said quietly, "it still has."

"All right, then." Dornie hitched his guns into a firmer seating on his thighs. "I'll be in to see you in a couple of days at most."

Burwick turned and walked away, and Dornie saw him swing easily to the saddle, but it was all very indistinct in the darkness. He stayed where he was, watching the darkness and listening to the slow steps of the horse. They had a funny sound—a very funny sound. When he walked back to the campfire, he was whistling "Green Grow the Lilacs."

The attack came at daybreak and the company had mustered twenty men, of whom two carried packages of dynamite. This was to be the final blow, to wipe out the squatters, once and for all.

Shortly before the arrival of Burwick, Keith and Dornie Shaw with Fessenden accompanying them had made a careful reconnaissance of the cañon from the rim. What they found pleased them enormously. It was obvious, once the crevasse had been located, that not more than two men could fire from it at once, and there was plenty of cover from the scattered boulders. In fact, they could get within throwing distance without emerging in the open for more than a few seconds at a time. Much of the squatters' field of fire would be ruined by their proximity to the ground and the rising of the boulders before them.

The attack started well with all the men moving out, and they made twenty yards into the cañon, moving fast. Here, the great slabs fallen from the slope of Yellow Butte crowded them together. And there the attack stopped. It stopped abruptly, meeting a withering wall of rifle fire, at point-blank range!

Tom Kedrick knew a thing or two about fighting, and he knew full well that his hide-out would in the long run become a deathtrap. He put himself in Keith's place, and decided what that man would do. Then he had his eight men, carrying fourteen rifles, slip like Indians through the darkness to carefully selected firing positions far down the cañon from where Keith would be expecting them.

Five of the attackers died in that first burst of fire, and, as the gun hands broke for cover, two more went down, and one dragged himself to the camp of the previous night with a shattered kneecap. He found himself alone. The wife of Taggart had begun it—the mighty blast of rifle fire completed it. The company fighters got out of the cañon's mouth, and as one man they moved for their horses, Keith among them and glad to be going. Dornie Shaw watched him mount up, and swung up alongside him. Behind them, moving carefully as if they were perfectly disciplined troops, the defenders of the cañon moved down, firing as they came. A horse dropped, and a man crawled into the rocks, then jumped up and ran. Dai Reid swung wide of the group and started after him.

Another went down before they got away, and Kedrick turned to his group. "Get your horses, men. The women will be all right. This is a job that needs finishing now."

A quarter of a mile away, Brokow spotted a horse, standing alone, and started for it. As he arose from the rocks, a voice called out from behind: "A minute!"

Brokow turned. It was only one man approaching him, the Welshman, Dai Reid. He stared at the man's Spencer, remembering his own gun was empty. He backed up slowly, his eyes haunted. "My rifle's empty," he said, "an' I've lost my Colt."

"Drop the rifle, then," Dai said quietly. "This I've been wanting, for guns be not my way."

Brokow did not understand, but he dropped his rifle. He was a big man, hulking and considered powerful. He watched in amazement as Reid placed his Spencer carefully on the ground, and then his gun belt. With bow-legged strides, the shorter man started for Brokow.

The outlaw stared, then started forward to meet Dai. As they drew near, he swung. His rock-like fist smashed Dai Reid flush on the chin, and Reid only blinked, then lunged. Twice more Brokow swung, blows filled with smashing panic born of the lack of effect of that first punch. Dai seemed unable to avoid them, and both connected solidly, and then his huge, big-knuckled hand grasped Brokow's arm and jerked him near. The hand slipped to the back of his head and jerked Brokow's face down to meet the rising of the Welshman's head. Stars burst before Brokow's eyes, and he felt the bone go in his nose. He swung wildly, and then those big hands gripped his throat and squeezed till Brokow was dead. Then Dai Reid dropped the outlaw to the sand, and, turning, he walked away. He did not notice the horse that stood waiting. It was a grulla.

In the headlong flight that followed the debacle in the cañon's mouth, only Lee Goff had purpose. The hard-bitten Montana gunman had stared reality in the face when Taggart's wife turned on him. It was only coincidence that she so resembled his own mother, long since dead of overwork in rearing seven boys and five girls on a bleak Montana ranch. He headed directly for Yellow Butte and the Taggart home. He did not dismount, only he stopped by the door and knocked gently. It opened, and he faced Mrs. Taggart, her eyes red now, from weeping. "Ma'am,' he said, "I guess I ain't much account, but this here's been too much. I'm driftin'. Will you take this here . . . as a favor to me?"

He shoved a thick roll of bills at her, his face flushing deep red. For an instant, she hesitated, and then she accepted the money with dignity. "Thanks, son. You're a good boy."

There's an old Mormon Trail across northern New Mexico into Colorado and Utah. Lee Goff's bald-faced sorrel stirred the dust on that road all the way across two states before its rider began to look the country over.

Behind him, had he known, Tom Kedrick was riding to Mustang. With him were Laredo Shad, Pit Laine, Dai Reid, Burt Williams, and the others. They made a tight, grim-faced little cavalcade, and they rode with their rifles across their saddle forks.

Due west of them, had they only known, another little drama was taking place, for the riders they followed were not all the riders who had abandoned the fight in the cañon. Two of them, Dornie Shaw and Colonel Loren Keith, had headed due west on their own. Both men had their own thoughts and their own ideas of what to do, and among other things Keith had decided that he had had enough. Whether the others knew it or not, they were through, and he was getting out of the country.

There was some money back there in Mustang, and, once he had that, he was going to mount up and head for California. Then let Ransome investigate. After a few years he would return to the East, and, if the subject ever came up, he would swear he had nothing to do with it, that he only represented them legally in the first steps of the venture.

What Dornie Shaw was thinking nobody ever guessed, and at this moment he had no thought at all in his mind. For his mind was not overly given to thought. He liked a few things, although he rarely drank, and seemed never to eat much. He liked a good horse and a woman with about the same degree of affection, and he had liked Sue Laine a good bit, but the woman who really fascinated him was Connie Duane, who never seemed aware that he was even alive. Most of all he liked a gun. When cornered or braced into a fight, he killed as naturally and simply as most men eat. He was a creature of destruction, pure and simple. Never in his life had he been faced with a man who made him doubt his skill, and never fought with anything but guns—and he vowed he never would.

The two rode rapidly and both were mounted well, so by the time Kedrick was leaving Yellow Butte and lining out for town, they reached the bank to Salt Creek Wash. Here Keith swung down to tighten his saddle cinch while his horse was drinking. After a moment, Dornie got down, too.

Absently Keith asked: "Well, Dornie, this breaks it, so where do you think you'll go now?"

"Why, Colonel," Shaw said softly, in his gentle

boy's voice, "I don't know exactly where I'm goin', but this here's as far as you go."

It took a minute for the remark to sink in, and then Keith turned, his puzzled expression stiffening into blank horror, then fear. Dornie Shaw stood negligently watching him, his lips smiling a little, his eyes opaque and empty. The realization left Loren Keith icy cold. Dornie Shaw was going to kill him. He had been an utter fool ever to allow this to happen. Why had he left the others and come off with Shaw? Why hadn't he killed him long since, from behind if need be, for the man was like a mad dog. He was insane, completely insane.

"What's on your mind, Shaw?" Without realizing it, he spoke as he might to a subordinate. Shaw was not conscious of the tone. He was looking at Keith's belt line. The colonel, he reflected, had been taking on a little weight here lately. "Why, just what I say. You've come as far as your trail takes you, Colonel. I can't say I'm sorry."

"Burwick won't like this. We're two of the men on whom he relies."

"Uh-huh, that's the way it was. It ain't now. Back yonder"—he jerked his head toward the butte—"he sort of implied he'd got hisself one too many partners." He shoved his hat back a little. "You want to try for your gun? It won't help you none, but you can try."

231

Keith was frightened. Every muscle within him seemed to have tightened until he could not move, yet he knew he was going to. But at the last, he had something to say, and it came from some deep inner conviction. "Kedrick will kill you, Dornie. He's going to win. He'll kill Burwick, too."

Suddenly he remembered something; it had been only a fleeting expression on Dornie Shaw's face, but, something. "Dornie?" he shot the word out with the force of desperation. "There behind you! The grulla!"

Shaw whirled, his face white, an almost animal-like fury on it. As he turned, Keith gasped hoarsely and triumphantly, and his gun swung up, but he had never coped with a fighter like Shaw. In the flashing instant that he whirled and found nothing behind him, Dornie hurled himself backward. The shot split wide the air where he had stood an instant before, and then Dornie himself fired from the ground. Fired once, then a second time.

Keith caught the bullet through the midsection, right where that extra weight had been gathering, and took the second one in the same place. He fell, half in the trickle of water that comprised Salt Creek. Feeding shells into his gun, Dornie Shaw stared down at the glazing eyes. "How did you know?" he asked sullenly. "How did you know?"

XV

Fessenden rode well forward in the saddle, his great bulk carried easily with the movement of the horse. His wide face was somber with thought and distaste. Like the others, the wife of Taggart had affected him as nothing else could have. He was a hard man who had done more than his share of killing, but he had killed men ruthlessly, thoughtlessly, men in mortal combat where he himself might die as easily. Several times before he had hired his gun, but each time in cattle or sheep wars or struggles with equals, men as gun-wise as he himself. Never before had he actually joined in a move to rob men of their homes. Without conscience in the usual sense, he had it in this case, for the men who moved West, regardless of their brand, were largely men in search of homes. Before, he had thought little of their fight. Several times he had helped to drive nesters from cattle range, and to him that was just and logical, for cows needed grass and people lived on beef, and most of the range country wasn't suited to farming, anyway. But in this case there was a difference, he now realized, thinking of it for the first time. In this case men were not being driven off for cattle, but only for profit. To many, the line was a fine one to draw;

to Fessenden and his like, once the matter was seen in its true light, that line became a gap, an enormous one.

Actually he rode in a state of shock. The victory Keith had wanted seemed so near. The taking of the few left in the cañon had seemed simple. His qualms against the use of dynamite he had shrugged off, if uncomfortably. Yet he had gone into the cañon with the others to get the thing over with, to get his money, and get out. And then, long before they expected it, came that smashing, thunderous volley, made more crashing by the close cañon walls, more destructive by the way the attackers were channeled by the boulders.

Shock started the panic, and distaste for the whole affair kept some of them, at least, on the move. Yet it was hard to believe that Clauson and Poinsett were dead, that Brokow had vanished, that Lee Goff was gone. For alone of the group, Goff had told Fessenden he was leaving. He had not needed to tell him why.

Behind him rode the Mixus boys, somber with disappointment at the failure of the attack. They had no qualms about killing, and no lines to draw even at the killing of women. They were in no true sense fighting men; they were butchers. Yet even they realized the change that had come over the group. What had become of Brokow or Goff they did not know, only that disintegration had set in, and these men had turned into a snarling pack of wolves, venting their fury and their hatred on each other.

Mustang was quiet when they rode into town. It was the quiet before the storm, and the town, like that cattle buyer who had turned back to Durango, sensed the coming fury of battle. No women were on the street, and only a few hardy souls loitered at the bars or card tables. The chairs before the St. James were deserted, and Clay Allison had ridden back to his home ranch, drunk and ugly.

An almost Sunday peace lay over the town when Fessenden drew up before the Mustang Saloon and swung down from his weary horse. Slapping his hat against his leg to beat off the dust, Fessenden stood like a great, shaggy bull and surveyed the quiet of the street. He was too knowing a Western man not to recognize the symptoms of disaster. Clapping his hat all awry upon his shaggy head, he shoved his bulk through the doors and moved to the bar.

"Rye," he said, his voice booming in the cavernous interior. His eyes glinted around the room, then back to the bartender.

That worthy could no longer restrain his curiosity. "What's happened?" he asked, swallowing.

A glint of irony came into the hard eyes of the gunman. "Them squatters squatted there for keeps," he said wryly, "an' they showed us they aim to stay put." He tossed off his drink. "All hell busted loose." Briefly he explained: "You'd 'a' figured there was a thousand men in that neck of the rocks when they opened up. The thing that did it was the unexpectedness of it, like steppin' on a step in the dark when it ain't there." He poured another drink. "It was that Kedrick," he said grimly. "When I seen him shift to the other side, I should've lit a shuck."

"What about Keith?"

"He won't be back."

They turned at the new voice, and saw Dornie Shaw standing in the doorway, smiling. Still smiling, he walked in and leaned against the bar. "Keith won't be back," he said. "He went for his gun out on Salt Creek."

The news fell into a silent room. A man at a table shifted his feet and a chair creaked. Fessenden wet his lips and downed his second drink. He was getting out of town, but fast.

"Seen that girl come in, short time back," the bartender said suddenly, "that Duane girl. Thought she'd gone over to the other side."

Dornie's head lifted and his eyes brightened, then shadowed. He downed his own drink and walked jauntily to the door. "Stick around, Fess. I'll be back." He grinned. "I'll collect for both of us from the old man."

The bartender looked at Fessenden. "Reckon he'll bring it if he does?"

The big gunman nodded absently. "Sure! He's

no thief! Why, that kid never stole a thing in his life. He doesn't believe in it. An' he won't lie or swear . . . but he'll shoot the heart out of you an' smile right in your face while he's doing it."

The show had folded. The roundup was over. There was nothing to do now but light out. Fessenden knew he should go, but a queer apathy had settled over him, and he ordered another drink, letting the bartender pour it. The liquor he drank seemed now to fall into a cavern without bottom, having no effect.

On the outskirts of town, Tom Kedrick reined in. "We'll keep together," he said quietly. "We want Keith, Shaw, Burwick, the Mixus boys, and Fessenden. There are about four others that you will know that I don't know by name. Let's work fast and make no mistakes. Pit, you take Dai and two men and go up the left side of the street, take no chances. Arrest them if you can, we'll try them, and"—his face was grim—"if we find them guilty, they'll have just two sentences . . . leave the country or hang. The Mixus boys and Shaw," he said, "will hang. They've done murder."

He turned in his saddle and glanced at the tall Texan. "Come on, Shad," he said, "we'll take two men and the right side of the street, which means the livery stable, the Saint James, and the Mustang." Kedrick glanced over at Laine. "Pit," he said, "if you run into Allison or Ketchum, better leave 'em alone. We don't want 'em."

Laine's face was grave. "I ain't huntin' 'em," he said grimly, "but if they want it, they can have it."

The parties rode into town and swung down on their respective sides of the street. Laredo grinned at Kedrick, but his eyes were sober. "Nobody wants to cross Laine today," he said quietly. "The man's in a killin' mood. It's his sister."

"Wonder what will happen when they meet?"

"I hope they don't," Shad said. "She's a right pretty sort of gal, only money crazy."

The two men with them stood hesitantly, waiting for orders. Both were farmers. One carried a Spencer .56, the other a shotgun. Shad glanced at them. "Let these *hombres* cover the street, Tom," he suggested. "You take the Saint James, an' I'll take the stable."

Kedrick hesitated. "All right," he agreed finally. "But take no chances, boy."

Laredo grinned and waved a negligent hand and walked through the wide door of the stable. Inside, he paused, cold and seemingly careless, but actually as poised and deadly as a coiled rattler. He had already seen Abe Mixus's sorrel pony and guessed the two dry-gulchers were in town. He walked on a step and saw the barrel of a rifle push through the hay.

He lunged right and dove into a stall, drawing his gun as he went, and ran full tilt into the other

238

Mixus! Their bodies smashed together, and Mixus, caught off balance, went down and rolled over. He came up, clawing for a gun. Laredo kicked the gun from under his hand and sent it spinning into the wide-open space between the rows of stalls.

With a kind of whining cry, Bean Mixus sprang after it, slid to his knees, and got up, turning. Laredo Shad stood, tall and dark, just within the stall, and, as Mixus turned like a rat cornered and swung his gun around, Laredo fired, his two shots slamming loudly in the stillness of the huge barn. Bean Mixus fell dead.

The rifle bellowed and a shot ripped the stall stanchion near Laredo's head. He lunged into the open, firing twice more at the stack of straw. The rifle jerked, then thundered again, but the shot went wild. Laredo dove under the loft where Abe Mixus was concealed, and fired two more shots through the roof over his head where he guessed the killer would be lying.

Switching his guns, he holstered the empty one and waited. The roof creaked some distance away, and he began to stalk the escaping Mixus, slipping from stall to stall. Suddenly a back door creaked and a broad path of light shot into the darkness of the stable. Laredo lunged to follow—too late.

The farmer outside with the shotgun was the man Sloan. As Abe Mixus lunged through the door to escape, they came face to face, at no more than twenty feet of distance. Abe had his rifle at his hip, and he fired. The shot ripped through the water trough beside Sloan, and the farmer squeezed off the left-hand barrel of his shotgun. The solid core of shot hit Mixus in the shoulder and neck, knocking him back against the side of the door, his neck and shoulder a mass of blood that seemed to well from a huge wound. He thought to get his gun up, but Sloan stepped around, remembering Bob McLennon's death and the deaths of Steelman and Slagle. The other barrel thundered and a sharp blast of flame stabbed at Abe Mixus. Smashed and dead, the killer sagged against the doorjamb, his old hat falling free, his face pillowed in the gray, blood-mixed dust.

Silence hung heavily in the wake of the shots. Into that silence Laredo Shad spoke. "Hold it, Sloan!" He stepped through the door, taking no glance at the fallen man. "The other one won't hang, either," he said. "They were both inside."

The two men drew aside, Sloan's face gray and sick. He had never killed a man before, and wanted never to again. He tried to roll a smoke, but his fingers trembled. Shad took the paper and tobacco from him and rolled it. The farmer looked up shame-facedly. "Guess I'm yaller," he said. "That sort of got me."

The Texan looked at him gloomily. "Let's hope

it always does," he said. He handed him the cigarette. "Try this," he told him. "It will make you feel better. Wonder how Kedrick's comin'."

"Ain't heard nothin'."

Pit Laine stood in a door across the street. "Everythin' all right?" he called.

"Yeah," the other farmer called back, "on'y you don't hafta look for the Mixus boys no more! They ain't gonna be around."

Captain Tom Kedrick had walked up the street and turned into the door of the St. James Hotel. The wide lobby was still, a hollow shell smelling faintly of old tobacco fumes and leather. The wrinkled clerk looked up and shook his head. "Quiet today," he said. "Nobody around. Ain't been no shootin' in days."

Guns thundered from down the street, then again and again, then silence, and the two solid blasts of the shotgun. Both men listened, and no further sound came. A moment later Pit Laine called out and the farmer answered. The clerk nodded. "Same town," he said. "Last couple of days I been wonderin' if I wasn't back in Ohio. Awful quiet lately," he said, "awful quiet."

Tom Kedrick walked down the hall and out the back door. He went down the weathered steps and stopped on the grass behind the building. There was an old, rusty pump there, and the sun was hot on the backs of the buildings. He walked over to the pump and worked the handle. It protested, whining and groaning at the unaccustomed work, and finally, despairing of rest, threw up a thick core of water that splashed in the wooden tub. When he had pumped for several minutes, Kedrick held the gourd dipper under the pump and let it fill. The water was clear and very cold. He drank greedily, rested, then drank again.

Far up the backs of the buildings at the opposite end of town, a man was swinging an axe. Kedrick could see the flash of light on the blade, and see the axe strike home, and a moment later the sound would come to him. He watched, then wiped the back of his hand across his mouth, and started along in back of the buildings toward the Mustang.

He moved with extreme care, going steadily, yet with every sense alert. He wore his .44 Russians and liked the feel of them, ready in his hands. The back door of the Mustang was long unpainted and blistered by many hot suns. He glanced at the hinges and saw they were rusty. The door would squeak. Then he saw the outside stairway leading to the second floor, and, turning, he mounted the stairs on tiptoe, easing through that door and walking down the hall.

In the saloon below, Fessenden had eliminated half a bottle of whiskey without destroying the deadening sense of futility that had come over him. He picked up a stack of cards and riffled them skillfully through his fingers, and there was no lack of deftness there. Whatever effect the whiskey had had, it was not on his hands. Irritated, he slammed the cards down and stared at the bartender. "Wish Dornie'd get back," he said for the tenth time. "I want to leave this town. She don't feel right today."

He had heard the shots down the street, but had not moved from the bar. "Some drunk cowhand," he said irritably.

"You better look," the bartender suggested, hoping for no fights in the saloon. "It might be some of your outfit."

"I got no outfit," Fess replied shortly. "I'm fed up. That stunt out there to Yeller Butte drove me off that range. I'll have no more of it."

He heard the footsteps coming down the hall from upstairs and listened to their even cadence. He glanced up, grinning. "Sounds like an Army man. Listen!"

Realization of what he had said came over him, and the grin left his face. He straightened, resting his palms on the bar. For a long moment, he stared into the bartender's eyes. "I knew it! I knew that *hombre* would . . ." He tossed off his drink. "Aw, I didn't want to leave town, anyway!"

He turned, moving back from the bar. He stood, spraddle-legged, like a huge grizzly, his big hands swinging at his hips, his eyes glinting upward at the balcony and the hall that gave onto it. The steps ceased, and Tom Kedrick stood there, staring down at him.

Neither man spoke for a full minute, while suspense gripped the watchers, and then it was Fessenden who broke the silence. "You lookin' for me, Kedrick?"

"For any of your crowd. Where's Shaw? And Keith?"

"Keith's dead. Shaw killed him back up on the Salt after you whipped us in the cañon. I dunno where he is now."

Silence fell once more and the two men studied each other. "You were among them at Chimney Rock, Fessenden," Kedrick said. "That was an ambush . . . dry-gulcher's stunt, Fess." Kedrick took another step forward, then side-stepped down the first step of the stairs which ran along the back wall until about six steps from the bottom, then, after crossing the landing, came down facing the room.

Fessenden stood there, swaying slightly on his thick, muscular legs, his brutal jaw and head thrust forward. "Aw, hell!" he said, and grabbed iron.

His guns fairly leaped from their holsters, spouting flame. A bullet smashed the top of the newel post at the head of the stairs, then ricocheted into the wall; another punctured a hole just behind Kedrick's shoulder. Tom Kedrick stepped down another step, then fired. His bullet turned Fessenden, and Kedrick ran lightly down four steps while Fessenden smashed two shots at him.

Kedrick dove headlong for the landing, brought up hard against the wall, and smashed another shot at the big man. It knocked a leg from under him, and he rolled over on his feet, colliding with the bar.

He had been hit twice, but he was cold sober and deadly. He braced himself and, with his left hand clinging to the bar, lifted his right and thumbed back the hammer. Kedrick fired two quick shots with his left gun. One ripped a furrow down the bar and hit Fessenden below the breast bone, a jagged, tearing piece of metal when it struck.

Fessenden fired again, but the bullet went wild, and his sixth shot was fired in desperation as he swung up his left-hand gun, dropping the right into his holster. Taking his time, feeling his life's blood running out of him, he braced himself there and took the gun over into his right hand. He was deliberate and calm. "Pour me a drink," he said.

The bartender, lying flat on his face behind the bar, made no move. Tom Kedrick stood on the edge of the landing now, staring at Fessenden. The big gunman had been hit three times, through the shoulder, the leg, and the chest, and he still stood there, gun in hand, ponderous and invulnerable.

The gun came up and Fessenden seemed to lean forward with it. "I wish you was Dornie," he said.

Kedrick triggered. The shot nailed Fessenden through the chest again. The big man took a fast step back, then another. His gun slipped from his hand, and he grabbed a glass standing on the bar. "Gimme a drink!" he demanded. Blood bubbled at his lips.

Tom Kedrick came down the steps, his gun ready in his hand, and walked toward Fessenden. Holding his gun level and low down with his right hand, Kedrick picked up the bottle with his left and filled the empty glass. Then he pulled over another empty glass and poured one for himself.

Fessenden stared at him. "You're a good man, Kedrick," he said, shaping the words patiently. "I'm a good man, too . . . on the wrong side."

"I'll drink to that." Kedrick lifted his glass, they clicked them, and Fessenden grinned crookedly over his.

"You watch that Dornie," he advised, "he's a rattler . . . mean." The words stumbled from his mouth and he frowned, lifting the glass. He downed his drink, choked on it, and started to hold out a big hand to Kedrick, then fell flat on his face. Holstering his gun, Tom Kedrick leaned over and gripped the big right hand. Fessenden grinned and died.

XVI

Connie Duane headed for Mustang only a short time after the survivors of the fight at Yellow Butte began to arrive. Restless, after leaving the men who were returning to the squatters' town, she had begun to think of what lay ahead, of Fred Ransome and the impending investigation, and of her uncle's part in it. All his papers as well as many of her own remained under lock in the gray stone house in Mustang, but if she was to get her own money back from Burwick, or was to clear any part of the blame from her uncle, she knew it must be done with those papers. She struck the old Mormon Trail and headed south. She was on that trail when the sun lifted, and she heard the distant sound of shots.

Turning from the trail, she reined her horse into the bed of Salt Creek and rode south, passing the point where only a short time later Loren Keith was to meet his death at the hands of Dornie Shaw. Once in Mustang, she believed she would be safe, and she doubted if anyone would be in the stone house unless it was Burwick, and she knew that he rarely left his chair.

Arriving in Mustang, she rode quickly up the street, then cut over behind the stone house and dismounted. She went into the house through the back door and went very quietly. Actually she need not have bothered, for Alton Burwick was not there. Making her way up the old stairs, she unlocked the door to the apartment she had shared with her uncle, and closed the door behind her.

Nothing seemed to have been disturbed. The blinds were drawn as she had left them and the room was still. A little dust had collected, and the light filtering in around the blinds showed it to her. Going to her trunk, she opened it and got out the ironbound box in which she carried her own papers. It was intact, and showed no evidence of having been tampered with. From the bottom of the trunk she took an old purse in which there were two dozen gold eagles, and these she changed to the purse she was now carrying.

Among other things there was an old pistol there, a huge, cumbersome thing. This she got out and laid on the table beside her. Then she found a Derringer seven-shot .22 caliber pistol her father had given her several years before he died, and she put it in the pocket of her dress.

Hurrying across the room, she went into the next room and began to go through her uncle's desk, working swiftly and surely. Most of his papers were readily available, and apparently nobody had made any effort to go through them, probably believing they contained nothing of consequence or that there would be plenty of time later. She was busy at this when she heard a horse walk by the house and stop near the back steps.

Instantly she stopped what she was doing and stood erect. The window here was partly open and she could hear the saddle creak very gently as whoever it was swung down. Then a spur jingled, and there was a step below, then silence.

"So? It's you."

Startled by the voice, Connie turned. Sue Laine stood behind her, staring with wide eyes. "Yes," Connie replied, "I came for some things of mine. You're Sue, aren't you?"

Without replying to the question, the girl nodded her head toward the window. "Who was that? Did you see?"

"No. It was a man."

"Maybe Loren has come back." Sue studied her, unsmiling. "How are they out there? Are they all right? I mean . . . did you see Pit?"

"Yes. He's unhappy about you."

Sue Laine flushed, but her chin lifted proudly. "I suppose he is, but what did he expect? That I was going to live all my life out there in that awful desert? I'm sick of it! Sick of it, I tell you!"

Connie smiled. "That's strange. I love it. I love it, and every minute I'm there, I love it more. I'd like to spend my life here, and I believe I will."

"With Tom Kedrick?"

Sue's jealousy flashed in her eyes, yet there

was curiosity, too. Connie noticed how the other girl studied her clothes, her face.

"Why . . . I . . . where did you ever get that idea?"

"From looking at him. What girl wouldn't want him? Anyway, he's the best of the lot."

"I thought you liked Colonel Keith?"

Sue's face flushed again. "I . . . I . . . thought I did, too. Only part of it was because Tom Kedrick wouldn't notice me . . . and because I wanted to get away from here, from the desert. But since then . . . I guess Pit hates me."

"No brother really hates his sister, I think. He'd be glad to see you back with him."

"You don't know him. If it had been anybody but someone associated with Alton Burwick, why . . ."

"You mean, you knew Burwick before?"

"Knew him?" Sue stared at her. "Didn't you know? Didn't he tell you? He was our stepfather."

"Alton Burwick?" Connie stared in amazement.

"Yes, and we always suspected that he had killed our father. We never knew, but my mother suspected later, too, for she took us and ran away from him. He came after us. We never knew what happened to mother. She went off one night for something and never came back, and we were reared by a family who just took us in."

A board creaked in the hall, and both girls were suddenly still, listening.

Guns thundered from the street of the town, and both girls stared at each other, holding their breath. There was a brief silence, then a further spattering of shots. Then the door opened very gently and Dornie Shaw stood there, facing the two girls.

He seemed startled at finding the two girls together, and looked from one to the other, his brown eyes bright, but now confused. Then he centered his eyes on Sue Laine. "You better get out," he said. "Keith's dead."

"Dead?" Sue gasped. "They . . . they killed him?"

"No, I did. Up on the Salt. He drew on me."

"Keith . . . dead." Sue was shocked.

"What about the others? Where are they?" Connie asked quickly.

Dornie turned his head sharply around and looked hard at her, a curious, prying gaze as if he did not quite know what to make of her. "Some of 'em are dead," he said matter-of-factly. "They whupped us. It was that Kedrick"—he spoke without emotion or shadow of prejudice as though completely indifferent—"he had 'em set for us an' they mowed us down." He jerked his head toward the street. "I guess they are finishin' up now. The Mixus boys an' Fessenden are down there."

"They'll be coming here," Connie said with conviction. "This is the next place."

"I reckon." He seemed indifferent to that, too. "Kedrick'll be the first one. Maybe"—he smiled—"the last one." He dug out the makings for a cigarette, glancing around the room, then back at Sue. "You git out. I want to talk to Connie."

Sue did not move. "You can talk to us both. I like it here."

As he touched his tongue to the paper, his eyes lifted and met hers. They were flat, expressionless. "You heard me," he said. "I'd hate to treat you rough."

"You haven't the nerve!" Sue flashed back. "You know what would happen to you if you laid hands on a woman in this country! You can get away with killing me, but this country won't stand for having their women bothered, even by a ratty little killer like you!"

Connie Duane was remembering the Derringer in her pocket and lowered her hand to her hip within easy grasp of the gun.

A sudden cannonade sounded, then a scattering of more shots. At that moment Kedrick was finally shooting it out with Fessenden. Dornie Shaw cocked an inquisitive ear toward the sound. "Gettin' closer," he said. "I ain't really in no hurry until Kedrick gets here."

"You'd better be gone before he does come." Connie was surprised at the confidence in her voice. "He's too much for you, and he's not half frightened like these others are. He'll kill you, Dornie."

He stared at her, then chuckled without humor. "Him? Bah! The man doesn't live who can outdraw Dornie Shaw! I've tried 'em all! Fess? He's supposed to be good, but he don't fool with Dornie! I'd shoot his ears off."

Calmly Connie dropped her right hand into her pocket and clutched the Derringer. The feel of it gave her confidence. "You had better go," she said quietly. "You were not invited here and we don't want you."

He did not move. "Still playin' it high an' mighty, are you? You've got to get over that. Come on, you're coming with me."

"Are you leaving?" Connie's eyes flashed. "I'll not ask you again!"

Shaw started to speak, but whatever it was he planned to say never formed into words, for Connie had her hand on the Derringer, and she fired from her pocket. Ordinarily she was a good shot, but she had never fired the gun from that position. The first bullet burned a furrow along Dornie Shaw's ear, notching it at the top, the second shot stung him along the ribs, and the third plowed into the table beside him.

With a growl of surprise, he dove through the door into the hall. Sue was staring at Connie. "Well, I never!" Her eyes dropped to the tiny gun that Connie had now drawn from her pocket. "Dornie Shaw! And with that! Oh, just wait until this gets around!" Her laughter rang out merrily, and despite herself Connie was laughing, too.

Downstairs, near the door, Dornie Shaw clutched his bloody ear and panted as though he had been running, his face twisting as he stared at his blood. Amazed, he scarcely noticed when Kedrick came up the steps, but, as the door pushed open, he saw him. For a fatal instant, he froze, then he grabbed for his gun, but he had lost his chance. In that split second of hesitation, Kedrick jumped. His right hand grasped Dornie's gun wrist, and Kedrick swung the gunman bodily around, hurling him into the wall. Shaw's body hit with a crash and he rebounded into a wicked right to the wind.

Shaw was no fighter with his hands, and the power of that blow would have wrecked many a bigger man. As it was, it knocked every bit of wind from the gunman's body, and then Kedrick shoved him back against the wall. "You asked me what I'd do, once, with a faster man. Watch this, Dornie!"

Kedrick lifted his right hand, and slapped the gunman across the mouth. Crying with fury, Shaw fought against the bigger man's grip while Kedrick held him flat against the wall, gripping him by the shirt collar, and slapped him, over and back. "Just a cheap killer," Kedrick said calmly.

"Somebody has already bled you a little. I'll do it for good."

He dropped a hand to Dornie's shirt and ripped it wide. "I'm going to ruin you in this country, Dornie. I'm going to show them what you are . . . a cheap, yellow-bellied killer who terrorizes men better than himself." He slapped Dornie again, then shoved him into the wall once more, and stepped back.

"All right, Shaw! You got your guns! Reach!"

Almost crying with fury, Dornie Shaw grabbed for his guns, but as he whipped them free, all his timing was wrecked by the events of the past few minutes. Kedrick's gun crashed and Shaw's right-hand gun was smashed from his hand. Shaw fired the left-hand gun, but the shot went wild, and Kedrick lunged, chopping down with his pistol barrel. The blow smashed Dornie Shaw's wrist and he dropped the gun with a yelp.

He fell back against the wall, trembling and staring at his hands. His left wrist was broken, his right thumb gone, and, where it had been, blood was welling.

Roughly Kedrick grabbed him and shoved him out the door. Shaw stumbled and fell, but Kedrick jerked him to his feet, unmindful of the gasps of the onlookers, attracted by the sounds of fighting. In the forefront of the crowd were Pit Laine, Dai Reid, and Laredo Shad, blinking with astonishment at the sight of the most feared gunman in the country treated like a whipped child.

Shaw's horse stood nearby, and Kedrick motioned to him. "Get on him . . . backward!"

Shaw started to turn and Kedrick lifted his hand and the gunman ducked instinctively. "Get up there! Dai, when he's up, tie his ankles together."

Dornie Shaw, befuddled by the whipping he had taken, scarcely aware of what was happening, lifted his eyes. He saw the grulla tied near the stone house. It was the last straw; his demoralization was complete.

Feared because of his deadly skill with guns and his love of killing for the sake of killing, he had walked a path alone, avoided by all, or catered to by them. Never in his life had he been manhandled as he had been by Tom Kedrick. His ego was shattered.

"Take him through the town." Kedrick's voice was harsh. "Show them what a killer looks like. Then fix up that thumb and wrist and turn him loose."

"Turn him loose?" Shad demanded. "Are you crazy?"

"No, turn him loose. He'll leave this country so far behind nobody will ever see him again. This is worse than death for him, believe me." He shrugged. "I've seen them before. All they need, that kind, is somebody to face them once who isn't afraid. He was fast and accurate with

256

his guns, so he developed the idea he was tough. Other folks thought the same thing. He wasn't tough. A tough man has to win and lose, he has to come up after being knocked down, he has to have taken a few beatings, and know what it means to win the hard way. Anybody can knock a man down. When you've been knocked down at least three times yourself, and then get up and floor the other man, then you can figure you're a tough *hombre*. Those smoke poles of Shaw's greased his path for him. Now he knows what he's worth."

The crowd drifted away and Connie Duane was standing in the doorway. Tom Kedrick looked up at her, and suddenly he smiled. To see her now, standing like this in the doorway, was like life-giving rain upon the desert, coming in the wake of many heat-filled days.

She came down the steps to him, then looked past him at Pit. "Your sister's upstairs, Pit. You'd better talk to her."

Laine hesitated, then he said stiffly: "I don't reckon I want to."

Laredo Shad drew deeply on his cigarette and squinted through the smoke at Laine. "Mind if I do?" he asked. "I like her."

Pit Laine was astonished. "After this?"

Shad looked at the fire end of his cigarette. "Well," he said, speaking seriously, "the best cuttin' horse I ever rode was the hardest to break.

257

Them with lot of git up an' go to 'em often make the best stock."

"Then go ahead." Pit stared after him. Then he said: "Tell her I'll be along later."

XVII

For three weeks there was no sign of Alton Burwick. He seemed to have vanished into the earth, and riders around the country reported no sign of him. At the end of that time three men got down from the afternoon stage and were shown to rooms in the St. James. An hour later, while they were at dinner, Captain Tom Kedrick pushed open the door and walked into the dining door. Instantly one of the men, a tall, immaculate man whose hair was turning gray at the temples, arose to meet him, hand outstretched. "Tom! Say, this is wonderful! Gentlemen, this is Tom Kedrick, the man I was telling you about. We served together in the war! Tom . . . Mister Edgerton and Mister Cummings."

The two men, one pudgy with a round, cheerful face, the other as tall as Ransome with gray mutton-chop whiskers acknowledged the introduction. When Kedrick had seated himself, they began demanding details. Quietly, and as concisely as possible, he told them his own story from his joining the company in New Orleans.

"And Burwick's gone?" Edgerton asked. He was the older man with the mutton-chop whiskers. "Was he killed?"

"I doubt it, sir," Kedrick replied. "He simply vanished. The man had a faculty for being out of the way when trouble came. Since he left, with the aid of Miss Duane and her uncle's papers, we managed to put together most of the facts. However, Burwick's papers have disappeared, or most of them."

"Disappeared?" Edgerton asked. "How did that happen?"

"Miss Duane tells me that when she entered the house before the final trouble with Shaw, she passed the office door and the place was undisturbed and the desk all in order. After the crowd had gone and when we returned, somebody had been rifling the desk and the safe."

"You imply that Burwick returned. That he was there then?"

"He must have been. Connie . . . Miss Duane . . . tells me that only he had the combination and that he kept all the loose ends of the business in his hands."

Cummings stared hard at Kedrick. "You say this Shaw fellow killed Keith? How do we know that you didn't? You admit to killing Fessenden."

"I did kill Fessenden. In a fair fight, before witnesses. I never even saw Keith's body after he was killed."

"Who do you think killed John Gunter?" Cummings demanded.

"My guess would be Burwick."

"I'm glad you're not accusing Keith of that," Cummings replied dryly.

"Keith wouldn't have used a knife," Kedrick replied quietly, "nor would he have attacked him from behind as was obviously the case."

"This land deal, Kedrick," Ransome asked, "where do you stand in it?"

"I? I don't stand at all. I'm simply not in it."

Cummings looked up sharply. "You don't stand to profit from it at all? Not in any way?"

"How could I? I own nothing. I have no holdings or claim to any."

"You said Burwick promised you fifteen percent?"

"That's right. But I know now that it was merely to appease me long enough to get me on the spot at Chimney Rock where I was to be killed along with the others. Burwick got me there, then rode off on the pretext that he wanted to look at a mineral ledge."

"How about this girl? The Duane girl?" Cummings asked sharply. "Does she stand to profit?"

"She will be fortunate to get back the money that her uncle invested."

"See, Cummings?" Ransome asked. "I told you Kedrick was honest. I know the man."

"I'll give my opinion on that later, after this investigation is completed. Not now. I want to go over the ground and look into this matter thoroughly. I want to investigate this matter of the disappearance of Alton Burwick, too. I'm not at all satisfied with this situation." He glanced down at the notes in his hand, then looked up. "As to that, Kedrick, wasn't Fessenden a duly elected officer of the law when you shot him? Wasn't he the sheriff?"

"Elected by a kangaroo election," Kedrick replied, "where the votes were counted by two officials who won. If that is a legal election, then he was sheriff."

"I see. But you do not deny that he had authority?"

"I do deny it."

Connie Duane was awaiting him when he walked back to his table. She smiled as he sat down, and listened to his explanation. She frowned thoughtfully. "Cummings? I think there is something in Uncle John's papers about him. I believe he was acting for them in Washington."

"That explains a lot." Kedrick picked up his coffee cup, then put it down abruptly, for Laredo Shad had come into the room, his face sharp and serious. He glanced around and, sighting Kedrick, hurried toward him, spurs jingling. Kedrick got to his feet. "What's wrong? What's happened?"

"Plenty! Sloan was wounded last night and Yellow Butte burned!"

"What?" Kedrick stared.

Shad nodded grimly. "You shouldn't have turned that rat loose. That Dornie Shaw."

Kedrick shook his head irritably. "I don't believe it. He was thoroughly whipped when he left here. I think he ran like a scared rabbit when he left, and, if he did want revenge, it would be after a few months, not so soon. No, this is somebody else."

"Who could it be?"

Tom's eyes met Connie's and she nodded, her eyes frightened. "You know who it could be. It could be Burwick."

Burwick had bothered him, getting away scot-free, dropping off the end of the world into oblivion as he had. Remembering the malignant look in the man's eyes, Kedrick became even more positive. Burwick had counted on this land deal, he had worked on it longer than any one of them, and it meant more to him.

"Shad," he said suddenly, "where does that grulla tie in? It keeps turning up, again and again. There's something more about all this than we've ever known, something that goes a lot deeper. Who rides the grulla? Why is it he has never been seen? Why was Dornie so afraid of it?"

"Was he afraid of the grulla?" Shad asked, frowning. "That doesn't figure."

"Why doesn't it? That's the question now. You know, that last day when I had Shaw thoroughly whipped, he looked up and saw something that scared him, yet something that I think he more than half expected. After he was gone down the street, I looked around, and there was nothing there. Later, I stumbled across the tracks of the grulla mustang. That horse was in front of the house during all the excitement!"

Frederic Ransome walked over to their table. "Cummings is going to stir up trouble," he said, dropping into a chair. "He's out to get you, Kedrick, and, if he can, to pin the killing of Keith on you, or that of Burwick. He claims your story is an elaborate build-up to cover the murder of all three of the company partners. He can make so much trouble that none of the squatters will get anything out of the land, and nothing for all their work. We've got to find Burwick."

Laredo lit a cigarette. "That's a tough one," he said, "but maybe I've got a hunch."

"What?" Kedrick looked up.

"Ever hear Burwick talk about the grulla?"

"No, I can't say that I did. It was mentioned before him once that I recall, and he didn't seem interested."

"Maybe he wasn't interested because he knowed all about it," Shad suggested. "That Burwick has me puzzled."

Connie looked up at him. "You may be right,

Laredo, but Pit and Sue Laine were Burwick's stepchildren and they knew nothing about the horse. The only one who seemed to know anything was Dornie Shaw."

Tom Kedrick got up. "Well, there's one thing we can do," he said. "Laredo, we can scout out the tracks of that horse and trail it down. Pick up an old trail, anything. Then just see where it takes us."

On the third day it began to rain. All week the wind had been chill and cold and the clouds had hung low and flat across the sky from horizon to horizon. Hunched in his slicker, Laredo slapped his gloved hands together and swore. "This finishes it!" he said with disgust. "It will wipe out all the trails for us."

"All the old ones anyway," Kedrick agreed. "We've followed a dozen here lately, and none of them took us anywhere. All disappeared on rock, or were swept away by wind."

"Escavada's cabin isn't far up this cañon," Shad suggested. "Let's hit him up for chow. It will be a chance to get warm, anyway."

"Know him?"

"Stopped in there once. He's half Spanish, half Ute. Tough old blister, an' been in this country since before the grass came. He might be able to tell us something."

The trail into the cañon was slippery and the

dull red of the rocks had been turned black under the rain. It slanted across the sky in a drenching downpour, and, when they reached the stone cabin in the corner of the hills, both men and horses were cold, wet, and hungry.

Escavada opened the door for them and waved them in. He grinned at them. "Glad to have company," he said. "Ain't seen a man for three weeks."

When they had stripped off their slickers and peeled down to shirts, pants, and boots, he put coffee before them and laced it with a strong shot of whiskey. "Warm you up," he said. "Trust you ain't goin' out again soon. Whiskey's mighty fine when a body comes in from the cold, but not if he's goin' out again. It flushes the skin up, fetches all the heat to the surface, then gives it off into the air. Man freezes mighty quick, drinkin' whiskey."

"You ever see a grulla mustang around, Escavada?" Laredo asked suddenly, looking up at the old man.

He turned on them, his eyes bright with malicious humor. "You ain't some of them superstitious kind, be you? Skeered o' the dark like? An' ghosts?"

"No," Kedrick said, "but what's the tie-up?"

"That grulla. Old story in this here county. Dates back thirty, forty years. Maybe further'n that. Sign of death or misfortune, folks say."

Laredo looked inquiringly at Kedrick, and Kedrick asked: "You know anything about it? That horse is real enough. We've both seen the grulla."

"So've I," the old man said. He dropped into a chair and grinned at them. His gray hair was sparse, but his eyes were alive and young. "I seen it many times, an' no misfortune come my way. Not unless you call losin' my shovel a misfortune." He hitched his chair nearer the woodpile and tossed a couple of sticks on the fire. "First I heerd of it was long ago. Old folks used to tell of a Spanish man in armor, ridin' a mouse-colored horse. He used to come an' go about the hills, but the story back of it seems to be that a long time back some such feller was mighty cruel to the Injuns. That story sort of hung around an' a body heered it ever' now and again until about fifteen, sixteen years back. Since then she's been mighty lively."

"You mean, you heard the story more since then?" Kedrick asked.

"Uh-huh. Started with a wagon train wiped out by Injuns up on the Salt. Ever' man jack o' them kilt dead . . . womenfolk, too, the story was. There was a youngster come off scot-free, boy about five or six years old. He crawled off into the brush, an', after, he swore them Injuns was led by a white man on a grulla horse, a white man in armor!"

"Wild yarn," Shad said, "but you can't blame the kid, imaginin' things after what he must've seen."

"He said that *hombre* in the armor went around with a long knife, an' he skewered ever' one of the bodies to make sure they was real dead. He said once that *hombre* looked right square at him, layin' in the brush, an' he was skeered like all git out, but must've been he wasn't seen, 'cause he wasn't bothered."

"An' this grulla has been seen since?" Shad asked. "Reg'lar?"

"Uh-huh, but never no rider close enough to say who or what. Sometimes off at a distance, sometimes just the horse, standin'. Most folks git clear off when they see that horse."

He got up and brought back the coffee pot. "Right odd you should ast me about him now," he commented. "Right odd."

Both men looked at him, and, sensing their acute interest, he continued. "Been huntin' here lately. Ketched me a few bees off the cactus an' mesquite, figurin' to start a beeline. Well, I got her started, all right, an' I trailed them bees to a place far south o' here. South an' west, actually. Most o' this country hereabouts is worked out of bees. I been at it so long I was workin' a good ways off. Well, my beeline took me over toward the Hogback. You know that place? She's a high-curvin' ridge maybe five or six hundred feet at the crest, but she rises mighty close to straight up for four hundred feet. Crawlin' up there to locate the cave them bees was workin' out of, I come on a cave like a cliff dwellin', on'y it wasn't. She was man-made, an' most likely in the past twenty years or so. What started me really lookin' was my shovel . . . the one I lost. She was right there on that ledge, so I knowed it hadn't been lost, but stole off me, so I began huntin' around. I found back inside this place it was all fixed up for livin'. Some grub there, blankets, a couple of guns, an' under some duffel in the corner an old-time breastplate an' helmet."

"You're serious?" Kedrick demanded incredulously.

"Sure as I'm alive! But"—Escavada chuckled—"that ain't the best of it. Lyin' there on the floor, deader'n last year's hopes, was a young fellow. He had a knife, an old-time Spanish knife that a feller in armor might have carried, an' it was skewered right th'ough him!"

"A young man . . . dead?" Kedrick suddenly leaned forward. "Anything odd about him? I mean . . . was he missing a thumb?"

Escavada stared. "Well, now, if that don't beat all! He was missin' a thumb, an' he was crippled up mighty bad in the other arm. Carried her in a sling."

"Dornie Shaw!" Laredo leaped to his feet. "Dornie Shaw, by all that's holy!"

"Shaw?" Escavada puckered his brows, his old eyes gleaming. "Now that's most odd, most odd! Shaw was the name o' that boy, the one who didn't git killed with the wagon train!"

Kedrick's face was a study. Dornie Shaw—dead! But if Dornie had been the boy from the wagon train, that would account for his superstitious fear of the grulla mustang. But to suppose that after all these years Dornie had been killed by the same man, or ghost if you believed in ghosts, that killed the rest of them so many years before was too ridiculous. It was, he thought suddenly, unless you looked at it just one way.

"Man can't escape his fate," Escavada said gloomily. "That boy hid out from that knife, but in the end it got him."

Kedrick got up. "Could you take us to that place, Escavada? Down there on the Hogback."

"I reckon." He glanced outside. "But not in this rain. Rheumatiz gits me."

"Then tell me where it is," Kedrick said, "because I'm going now!"

They were crossing the head of Coal Mine Creek when Laredo saw the tracks. He drew up suddenly, pointing. The tracks of a horse, well shod. "The grulla," Kedrick said grimly. "I'd know those tracks anywhere."

They pushed on. It was late and the pelting

rain still poured down upon their heads and shoulders. The trails were slippery, and dusk was near. "We'd better find us a hole to crawl into," Shad suggested. "We'll never find that horse in this weather."

"By morning the tracks will be gone, and I've a hunch we'll find our man right on that cliff dwelling where Escavada saw Dornie's body."

"Wonder how Dornie found the place."

"If what I think is right," Kedrick replied, wiping the rain from his face, "he must have run into an old friend and been taken there to hide out. That old friend was the same rider of the grulla that killed his family and friends with the wagon train, and, when he saw that armor, he knew it."

"But what's it all about?" Shad grumbled. "It don't make sense! An' no horse lives that long."

"Sure not. There may have been half a dozen grullas in that length of time. This man probably tried to capitalize on the fears of the Indians and Mexicans who live up that way to keep them off his trail. We'll probably find the answer when we reach the end of our ride."

The Hogback loomed, black and ominous, before them. The trail, partly switchback and partly sheer climb, led over the sharp, knife-like ridge. They mounted, their horses laboring heavily at the steep and slippery climb. Twice Tom Kedrick saw the tracks of the grulla on the trail, and in neither case could those tracks have been more than an hour old.

Kedrick glanced down when they saw the opposite side, then dismounted. "This one is tricky," he said grimly. "We'd better walk it."

Halfway down, lightning flashed, and in the momentary brightness Laredo called out: "Watch it, Tom! High, right!"

Kedrick's head jerked around just as the rifle boomed. The bullet smacked viciously against the rock beside him, spattering his face with splinters. He grabbed for his gun, but it was under his slicker. The gun boomed again, five fast shots, as fast as the marksman could work the lever of his rifle.

Behind Tom Kedrick the anguished scream of a wounded horse cut the night and Shad's warning yell was drowned in the boom of the gun again, and then he flattened against the rock barely in time to avoid the plunging, screaming horse! His own Appaloosa, frightened, darted down the trail with the agility of a mountain goat. The rifle boomed again, and he dropped flat.

"Shad? You all right?"

There was a moment before the reply, then it was hoarse, but calm. "Winged me, but not bad."

"I'm going after him. You all right?"

"Yeah. You might help me wrap this leg up."

Sheltered by the glistening rain-wet rock, with gray mist swirling past them on the high ridge of the Hogback, Kedrick knelt in the rain, and, shielding the bandage from the rain with a slicker, he bound the leg. The bullet had torn through the flesh, but the bone was not broken.

XVIII

When the wound was bandaged, Kedrick drew back into the shelter of the slight overhang and stared about. Ahead and below them was a sea of inky blackness. Somewhere down that mountain would be their horses, one probably dead or dying, the other possibly crippled. Around them all was night and the high, windy, rain-wet rocks. And out there in the darkness a killer stalked them, a killer who could at all of three hundred yards spot his shots so well as to score two hits on a target seen only by a brief flash of lightning. Next time those shots could kill. And there was no doubt about it. Now the situation was clear. It was kill or be killed.

"Sure," Laredo said dryly, "you got to get him, man. But you watch it. He's no slouch with that Spencer!"

"You've got to get off this ridge," Kedrick insisted. "The cold and rain up here will kill you."

"You leave that to me," Shad replied shortly. "I'll drag myself down the trail an' find a hole to crawl into down on the flat below this Hogback. Might even find your palouse down there. You got grub an' coffee in those saddlebags?"

"Yeah, but you'd better not try a fire until I come back."

Shad chuckled. "Make sure you come back. I never did like to eat alone."

Slipping his hands under his slicker through the pockets, Tom gripped his guns. His rifle, of course, was in his saddle scabbard. He was going to have to stalk a skilled killer, a fine marksman, on his own ground in absolute darkness with a handgun. The killer had a Spencer .56.

Lightning flashed, but there was no more shooting. Somewhere out there the killer was stalking them. He would not give up now, or retreat. This, for him, was a last stand unless he killed them both. His hide-out now was known, and, if they escaped, he would no longer be safe. That he did not intend to be driven from the country was already obvious by the fact that he had stayed this long.

Kedrick crawled out, using a bush to cover his movement, and then worked along the windy top of the ridge toward a nest of boulders he had seen ahead of him by the lightning flash. The wind whipped at his hat, and flapped the skirt of his slicker. His right-hand gun was drawn, but under the slicker.

He crawled on. Lightning flashed and he

flattened out on the rocks, but the Spencer bellowed, the bullet smashing his eyes and mouth full of gravel. Rolling over, he held his fire, spitting and pawing desperately at his blinded eyes.

There was no sound but the wind and rain. Then in the distance, thunder roared and rumbled off among the peaks, and, when the lightning flashed again, he looked out along the high ridge of the Hogback. Lashed by the driving rain, its rocks glistened like steel under clouds that seemed a scarce arm's length above Kedrick's head. Mist drifted by him, touching his wet face with a ghostly hand, and the little white skeletons of long-dead pines pointed their sharp and bony fingers toward the sky.

Rain pelted against his face, and he cowered, fearing the strike of a bullet at each flash of lightning, smelling the brimstone as the lightning scarred the high ridge with darting flame. He touched his lips with his tongue and stared until his eyes ached with strain. His mouth was dry and his stomach empty, and something mounted within him. Fear? Panic? He could stay still no longer. With infinite patience, he edged forward, working his way a little over the edge of the ridge toward the hulking black clumps of some juniper, ragged trees whipped to agonized shapes by generations of wind.

There was no sound but the storm, no sight of

anything. He moved on, trying to estimate how far away the cliff house would be, to guess if he could reach it first or get between it and the killer out there. Flame stabbed the night and something burned sharply along his shoulders. He let go everything and rolled, went crashing down a dozen feet before he brought up in a tangle of dead limbs.

But the killer was not waiting. He loomed suddenly dark on the crest, and, crouching like a hunted animal, every instinct alert. Kedrick fired! The dark figure jerked hard, and then the Spencer bellowed. The bullet plastered a branch near him, and Kedrick knew that only his own shot had saved his life. He fired again, and then deliberately hurled himself backward into the night, falling, landing, crawling. He got to his feet and plunged into the absolute darkness, risking a broken limb or a bad fall, anything to get the distance he needed. Then lightning flashed, and, as if by magic, the Spencer boomed. How the man had followed his plunging careen he could not know, but he felt the stab and slam of the bullets as they smashed about him. This man was shooting too close. He couldn't miss long.

His shoulders burned, but whether that shot had been a real wound or a mere graze he did not know. Something fluid trickled down his spine, but whether it was rain water through the slit coat or his own blood, he could not guess.

He moved back, circling. Another shot, but this slightly to his left. Quickly he moved left and a shot smacked right near where he had been standing. The killer was using searching fire now, and he was getting closer.

Kedrick moved back, tripped and fell, and bullets laced the air over him. Evidently the man had a belt full of ammunition, or his pockets stuffed. Kedrick started to rise, but his fingers had found a hard smoothness, not of rock, but of earth and gravel! Carefully he felt about in the darkness. The path! He was on a path, and no doubt the path to the cliff house.

He began to move along it, feeling his way carefully. Once, off to his left, he heard a rock roll. He took a chance and fired blind, then rolled over three times and felt the air split apart as the shots slammed the ground where he had been. He fired again, then again, always moving.

Lightning flashed, and he saw a hulking thing back on the trail the way he had come, a huge, glistening thing, black and shining. Flame sprang from it, and he felt the shock of the bullet, then steadied himself and fired again.

Deliberately then, he turned and worked his way down the path. Suddenly he felt space before him, and found the path here took a sharp turn. Another step and he might have plunged off! How near was his escape he knew in another instant when lightning flashed and he saw far below him the gray white figure of the Appaloosa standing in the rain.

He worked his way down the cliff, then found a ledge, and in a moment his hands found the crude stone bricks of the cliff house. Feeling his way along it, he felt for the door, and then, pushing it open, he crawled into the inner darkness and pushed the door shut behind him.

After the lashing of wind and rain the peace seemed a miracle. Jerking off his soaking hat, he tossed it aside, and threw off the slicker. There was a chance the killer would not guess that he knew of this place, and undoubtedly, had he not known, he would have passed it in the darkness and storm. Working his way along the floor, he found a curtain dividing this from an inner room. He stepped through it and sat down hard on the bunk. Feeling for his left-hand gun, he found the holster empty, and he had fired five shots with his right gun. Suddenly the curtain stirred and there was a breath of wind, then it vanished. The killer was in the other room! He had come in!

Kedrick dared not rise for fear the bed would creak, but he heard a match strike, and then a candle was lighted. Feet shuffled in the other room. Then a voice. "I know you're in there, Kedrick. There's water on the floor in here. I'm behind a piece of old stone wall that I use for a sort of table. I'm safe from your fire. I know there's no protection where you are. Throw your guns out and come with your hands up! If you don't, I'm going to open fire an' search every inch of that room!"

Over the top of the blanket curtain, which was suspended from a pole across the door, Tom Kedrick could see the roof in the other room. The cave house was actually much higher than need be; evidently the killer had walled up an overhang or cave. Kedrick could see several heavy cedar beams that had served to support a ceiling, now mostly gone. If that was true in the other room, it might be true in his, also.

He straightened to his feet, heard a sudden move, then fired! From the other room came a chuckle. "Figured that would draw fire! Well, one gun's empty. Now toss out the other an' come out. You haven't a chance!"

Kedrick did not reply. He was reaching up into the darkness over his head, feeling for the beams. He touched one, barely touched it, then reached up with both hands, judging the distance he had to jump by the width of the beams in the other room. What if it were old and would not support his weight? He had to chance that.

He jumped, his fingers hooked well over the edge, and soundlessly he drew himself up. Now Kedrick could see into the lighted room, but he could not locate the killer. The voice spoke again. "I'm giving you no more time, Kedrick. Come out or I start to shoot! Toss that other gun first!"

Silence lay in the room, a silence broken by the sudden bellow of a gun! The killer fired, emptied a six-gun, then emptied another. Tom Kedrick waited, having no idea how many guns the man had, or what he might have planned for. Then six more carefully spaced shots were fired, one of them ricocheting dangerously close to Kedrick's head.

A long pause, and then a sound of movement. "All right, if you're alive in there now, you got a shot comin', but if you want to give up, you can. I sort of want you alive." Suddenly the blanket was jerked from its moorings, and Alton Burwick stood in the opening, a gun gripped in his fist, ready to fire. Kedrick made no sound, and the man stared, then rushed into the room. Almost whining with fury, he jerked Kedrick's hat from the bed, then the slicker, and, as the latter fell to the floor, with it fell Kedrick's other pistol, which falling from the holster had hooked into some tear in the slicker. He stared at it furiously, and then jerked the bed aside. Almost insane with fury, he searched, unbelieving and whining like an angry hound on a trail.

He stopped, his pent-up fury worn away, and stood there, his chest heaving with his exertions, his fist still gripping the pistol. "Gone!

279

Gone!" he cried, as if bereft. "When I had him right here!"

Kedrick's fingers had found a tiny sliver of wood, and deliberately he snapped it against Burwick's cheek. The fat man jerked as if stung, then looked up. Their eyes met, and slowly he backed away, but now he was smiling. "Oh, you're a smart one, Kedrick! Very smart! Too bad it couldn't have been you with me instead of that weakling Keith! All front and show, but no bottom to him, no staying quality! But"—he sighed—"I've got you anyway, and you'll suffer for what you've done." He scooped Kedrick's other pistol from the floor and backed away. "All right, get down!"

Kedrick dropped to the floor, and the fat man waved irritably at the gun he clutched. "No use to bluff. That's empty. Throw it down!"

"What's it all about, Burwick?" Tom asked suddenly. "Why this place? The armor? What about Dornie Shaw?"

"Ah? How did you know about that? But no matter, no matter." He backed to the wall, watching Kedrick and holding the gun. "Why, it was gold, boy! Gold, and lots of it! It was I stirred those Indians up to attacking that caravan. I wanted the gold they carried, and most of it belonging to Dornie's pa. I knew about it. Followed them from Dodge. Knew when they drew it from the bank there, and how much. They fooled me, though. When the Indians hit, they'd buried it somewhere. It could have been a lot of places, that was the trouble.

"They might have buried it sooner, somewhere else along the trail. I've dug and I've hunted, but I've never found it. Maybe I will someday, but nobody else is going to! Wondered why I wanted the land? Profit, sure. But I wanted this place, a couple of sections in here, all for myself. Figured on that, working it out somehow. The gold's somewhere between here and Thieving Rock. Has to be."

Kedrick nodded. "That clears up a lot of things. Now you drop that gun, Burwick, and come as my prisoner."

Burwick chuckled fatly. "Try to bluff me? I'd've expected that from you. Nervy one, huh? Bet you got that Connie Duane, too. By the Lord Harry, there's a woman! No scare to her. Not one bit. Drop your gun, boy, or I'll put my first bullet through your kneecap."

He was going to shoot, and Tom Kedrick knew it. Coolly he squeezed off his own shot, an instant faster. He shot for the gun hand, but the bullet only skinned the thumb knuckle and hit Burwick in the side. The fat man jerked and his face twisted, and he stared at the gun, lifting his own. Coolly Kedrick fired again, then again. The bullets struck with an ugly smack, and Burwick wilted, the gun going from his limp fingers to the

281

floor. Kedrick stepped in and caught him, easing him down. The flabby cheeks were suddenly sagging and old.

Bitterly the man stared upward at him. "What happened? That . . . that . . . ?"

"The gun was a Walch twelve-shot pistol," Tom explained. "I started carrying them a few days ago, replacing the Forty-Four Russians."

Burwick stared at him, no hatred in his eyes. "Smart," he said. "Smart! Always one trick better than me, or anybody. You'll . . . do, boy."

On the streets of Mustang the sun was warm after the rain. Tom Kedrick, wounded again but walking, stood beside Connie Duane. Shad was grinning at them. "Look mighty fine in that tailored suit, Tom. You goin' to be gone long?"

"Not us. We'll be married in Santa Fe, and then we're headin' for the Mogollons and that ranch."

"Seems a shame not to hunt for that gold," Laredo complained. "But, anyway, the real treasure was that box full of Burwick's papers. Sure made Cummings hunt his hole. But I do regret that gold."

"I don't," Connie replied. "It's caused too much trouble. Alton Burwick spent his life and a good many other lives after it. Let it stay where it is. Maybe a better man will find it, who needs it more than we do!"

"Gosh," Laredo said suddenly, "I got to light a shuck. I'm late to meet Sue. So long, then!" They watched him go, waiting for the stage.

Everything was quiet in Mustang—three whole days without a killing.

ABOUT THE AUTHOR

Louis Dearborn LaMoore (1908-1988) was born in Jamestown, North Dakota. He left home at fifteen and subsequently held a wide variety of jobs although he worked mostly as a merchant seaman. From his earliest youth, L'Amour had a love of verse. His first published work was a poem, "The Chap Worth While," appearing when he was eighteen years old in his former hometown's newspaper, the *Jamestown Sun*. L'Amour wrote poems and articles for a number of small circulation arts magazines all through the early 1930s and, after hundreds of rejection slips, finally had his first story accepted, "Anything for a Pal" in *True Gang Life* (10/35). He returned in 1938 to live with his family where they had settled in Choctaw, Oklahoma, determined to make writing his career. He wrote a fight story bought by Standard Magazines that year and became acquainted with editor Leo Margulies who was to play an important role later in L'Amour's life. "The Town No Guns Could Tame" in *New Western* (3/40) was his first published Western story.

During the Second World War L'Amour was drafted and ultimately served with the U.S. Army Transportation Corps in Europe. However, in the two years before he was shipped out, he managed to write a great many adventure stories for Standard Magazines. The first story he published in 1946, the year of his discharge, was a Western, "Law of the Desert Born" in *Dime Western* (4/46). A call to Leo Margulies resulted in L'Amour's agreeing to write Western stories for the various Western pulp magazines published by Standard Magazines, a third of which appeared under the byline Jim Mayo, the name of a character in L'Amour's earlier adventure fiction.

L'Amour's first Western novel under his own byline was *Westward the Tide* (World's Work, 1950). L'Amour sold his first Western short story to a slick magazine two years later, "The Gift of Cochise" in *Collier's* (7/5/52). Robert Fellows and John Wayne purchased screen rights to this story from L'Amour for $4,000 and James Edward Grant, one of Wayne's favorite screenwriters, developed a script from it. L'Amour retained the right to novelize Grant's screenplay, which differs substantially from his short story. *Hondo* (Fawcett Gold Medal, 1953) by Louis L'Amour was released on the same day as the film, *Hondo* (Warner, 1953), with a first printing of 320,000 copies.

With *Showdown at Yellow Butte* (Ace, 1953) by Jim Mayo, L'Amour began a series of short Western novels that could be doubled with other short novels by other authors in Ace Publishing's paperback two-fers. *Heller With a Gun* (Fawcett Gold Medal, 1955) was the first of a series of original Westerns L'Amour had agreed to write under his own name following the success for Fawcett of *Hondo*. The great turn in L'Amour's fortunes came about when he was signed by Bantam Books. By 1962 he was writing three original paperback novels a year. *All* of his Bantam Western titles came to be continuously kept in print.

There are also several characteristics in purest form that, no matter how diluted they ultimately would become, account in largest measure for the loyal following Louis L'Amour won from his readers: the young male narrator who is in the process of growing into manhood and who is evaluating other human beings and his own experiences; a resourceful frontier woman who has beauty as well as fortitude; a strong male character who is single and hence marriageable; and the powerful, romantic, strangely compelling vision of the American West which invests L'Amour's Western fiction and makes it such a delightful escape from the cares of a later time.

Books are
produced in the
United States
using U.S.-based
materials

Books are printed
using a revolutionary
new process called
THINKtech™ that
lowers energy usage
by 70% and increases
overall quality

Books are
durable and
flexible
because of
Smyth-sewing

Paper is
sourced using
environmentally
responsible
foresting methods
and the
paper is acid-free

Center Point Large Print
600 Brooks Road / PO Box 1
Thorndike, ME 04986-0001 USA

(207) 568-3717

US & Canada:
1 800 929-9108
www.centerpointlargeprint.com